SO-ASY-792

G. Raymond Carlson

THE ACTS STORY

Gospel Publishing House
Springfield, Missouri

02-0913

Contents

© 1978 by the Gospel Publishing House, Springfield, Missouri 65802.
Adapted from Acts by Emil Balliet, © 1972 by the Gospel Publishing
House. All rights reserved. Library of Congress Catalog Card Number
78-57178. ISBN: 0-88243-913-8.

A Teacher's Guide for individual or group study with this book is
available from the Gospel Publishing House. Order No. 32-0184.

1   The Church Begins

Read: Acts 1:1 to 2:4

Do you have a "doctor's" book in your home?
Many people have some kind of a family medicine
book for ready reference. There's a book written by a
physician-turned-author that is available at most any
store and is really worthwhile. You can read it in less
than 2 hours.

Written about 1900 years ago, this book is relevant
to today's society. Translated into hundreds of languages, it belongs to a larger Book that continues to
be an all-time best-seller.

This book, called *The Acts of the Apostles,* was
written by Luke the "beloved physician" as a sequel
to the Gospel bearing his name. That's clear from a
comparison of the opening verses of both Books. In
his Gospel, Luke traces the earthly ministry of Jesus;
in Acts, he traces the work of Christ from heaven
through the Holy Spirit in the lives of believers.

To Jews . . . To Gentiles

The Book of Acts is a very important historical
record dealing with the establishing of the Church.
Peter and Paul were the two great leaders used by
the Holy Spirit, and the Book of Acts is occupied
mostly with the ministry of these two apostles. Chapters 1 through 12 deal with the establishment of the
Church among the Jews in Jerusalem and the con-

tiguous areas, which were largely under the leadership of Peter. The balance of the Book (chapters 13 through 28) deals with the establishment of the Church among the Gentiles, which was almost entirely under Paul's leadership from Antioch, the new center of missionary activity.

From Jerusalem to Rome

The Book opens with the preaching of the gospel in Jerusalem, the religious center of the Jewish nation, and closes with the preaching in Rome, the center of world power in that day. The key verse, "But ye shall receive power, after that the Holy Ghost is come upon you: and ye shall be witnesses unto me both in Jerusalem, and in all Judea, and in Samaria, and unto the uttermost part of the earth" (Acts 1:8), finds fulfillment. The work spread from Jerusalem to the "uttermost parts."

Words Concerning Deeds

Acts is called the pivotal Book of the New Testament. It provides the link between the Gospels and the Epistles. Acts supplies the sequel to the Gospels and the historical background to the Epistles.

The seeds of doctrine are born in Acts and developed later in the Epistles. Acts gives us doctrine in practice; it is exemplified in the lives of the believers. The Epistles develop the systematic statement of doctrine.

Principles and Patterns Laid Down

Read Acts and you will find great principles and patterns for the Church. Expansion, revival, missionary endeavor, growth—they are all pictured. Persecution and adversity are met and conquered. Church government is set forth. Prayer meetings are reported and sermons are recorded. The activity of

Christ by the Holy Spirit through believers is fascinating reading.

The Book has 28 chapters. There is no formal conclusion because the story hasn't really ended. The "29th chapter" continues to this day. While the Book has been labeled The Acts of the Apostles, a more correct title would be "The Acts of the Holy Spirit."

The preachers and witnesses in Acts had a vital awareness of their resurrected Lord. They served the living Christ. And He had given them the promised Comforter. Luke gives the thrilling account of the growing Apostolic Church and the secret of apostolic Christianity, namely, the living Christ and the dynamic ministry of the Holy Spirit.

The first chapter of Acts is packed with important information. Jesus had been raised from the dead. He was about to ascend to the Father. His followers were soon to be empowered by the Holy Spirit for the world-shaking task of proclaiming the gospel.

The New Certainty

The crucifixion of Christ had left the disciples disillusioned. Their hopes and dreams lay shattered in the cold, cold grave. And then they were shocked by the astonishing discovery of an empty grave. Stunning events hurtled around them with perplexing rapidity. Christ's resurrection was as unexpected as His death.

Many Infallible Proofs

Belief did not come easy. But for 40 days Jesus appeared before the disciples and by many "infallible proofs" assured them He was really alive. He proved to them the reality of His resurrection. The most stupendous fact of history had actually happened! Their Christ had crushed the grasp of death;

He had emerged triumphant, conquering death, the curse of sin, and Satan, the cause of it all.

Death had not ended His activity; it was to continue from the right hand of His Father's throne. But before He took His lofty place and His glorified position, He undertook the task of stamping His resurrection indelibly on the minds of His disciples and, therefore, on His church. The gaping wounds presented to sight and touch, the sharing of food—all was experiential proof. They *saw* Him; they *talked* with Him; they *ate* with Him. The proofs were incontestable. Added to all this was His unfolding of Scripture with reference to His death and resurrection.

All doubts disappeared. He was not an apparition. This was no hallucination. Truly He was Lord and Master. Imagine their delight. What conversations they must have had. What assurance! What joy!

The New Mission

The disciples looked on their Master as the Messiah who would restore the kingdom of Israel (v. 6). That hope had been shattered with His death (Luke 24:21). Now His resurrection gave new impetus to that hope. Surely nothing could now stand in the way of His triumphant march to a throne in Jerusalem and world dominion.

Their question regarding the restoration of the kingdom (Acts 1:6) did not receive a direct answer. Jesus did affirm that Israel's kingdom hope would be realized, but not at that time. He did not deny the validity of their dream, but He did give them a clearer understanding of the sequence of events that must precede the fulfillment of the messianic promise of the kingdom.

New Concern Becomes Apparent

Christ gave them to understand that the kingdom and its restoration should no longer be the focus of their concern. They must learn that their Lord had a major task at hand in which their efforts were required. The timetable of the kingdom must be left in the Father's hand (v. 7). They were to preach the gospel (Matthew 28:19; Acts 1:8), and the Lord was going to build His church (Matthew 16:18). The publishing of the good news was now their calling; they were to gird themselves for that task.

The New Equipment

"Ye shall be witnesses unto me." This is the grand and glorious occupation of the Church. Not learning, reformation, political power, ecclesiastical authority and order, or social action, but making Christ known in the simplicity and power of the gospel.

The commission given to the disciples to witness, beginning in Jerusalem and extending then to Judea, Samaria, and the whole world, was staggering. The task would have to be done in the face of opposition by men and demons.

The idea of being a humble witness doesn't appeal to people in general. Most prefer to rule rather than witness. Witnessing is to be in the will of God and never an activity of the flesh based on human whim or fancy.

Divine Enablement Is Needed

Human ability is never adequate for a divine task. Many of those who were present as Jesus gave His parting instructions had sat under His ministry for some time. Several of them had received intensive training for 3 years. Never had there been a better teacher. But even such excellent schooling had not

7

sufficiently equipped them for the assignment. They needed supernatural power.

We agree the task is too great for us. But there is no excuse for a powerless witness. We need the supernatural today as did those who gathered in the Upper Room. We need the person and the gifts of the Holy Spirit. God's work is accomplished "not by might, nor by power, but by my Spirit, saith the LORD of hosts" (Zechariah 4:6).

The New Perspective

For 40 days Jesus had ministered in person to His followers following His resurrection. Their discouragement had fled; their faith had been assured; their understanding had been opened. Up to this time they had lived and worked—seeing their Master in the flesh. For this reason His death had brought everything to a standstill. His resurrection didn't restore the old perspective, but prepared them for a new one. There was no doubt that He was alive, but now they would come to know Him as being "at the right hand of God."

The Divine Lift-off

Jesus' earthly ministry was finished. Suddenly before the wondering eyes of His disciples He "was taken up." A cloud received Him out of their sight. They were alone, and yet not alone. They had the assurance He was alive.

Altogether there are about 120 references to the Ascension in the New Testament. Surprisingly little detail is given. Among the references are Acts 1:9-11; Ephesians 4:8-10; and Hebrews 1:3.

The Ascension Brings Assurance

The Ascension is the complement of the Incarnation. The incarnate Son died for us, He was raised for our justification, and He was accepted back to the right hand of the Father. Thus, in the Ascension we have a threefold assurance of *atonement, acceptance,* and *authority.* We can face our past, present, and future in perfect confidence. The resurrected Christ is now appearing in the heavens as our *Mediator.* His ascension was the climaxing event of His entire earthly career (v. 9).

While the disciples watched their Lord's lift-off into the heavens, two angels confirmed His promise to return (v. 11). When He returns, and only then, will believers experience resurrection. We will have glorified bodies.

The New Experience

The disciples realized their Lord would come again and in view of that they must carry out the commission He had given them. They were not aimless sky-gazers, helpless in the wake of His absence. He was alive and had commanded them to "wait for the promise of the Father." They could *look up* to their Lord on His throne; they could *look forward* to His return in the clouds; they must *look out* on the throngs that needed their witness. But first they must obey His command to receive His promised power.

Jesus gave the disciples instructions for immediate action. It was clear and simple: They must wait in Jerusalem. In obedience they gathered in an upper room. Before Gethsemane they had been ministered to in an upper room. Following the Crucifixion they had hidden in fear in the city. Now in obedience they awaited a new experience in an upper room. There they remained in prayer and supplication in one accord. During this time a successor to Judas Iscariot, the betrayer of the Lord Jesus, was chosen from the group (v. 26).

Then It Happened

Suddenly! For 10 days they had prayed. For 10 days they had waited. The Day of Pentecost dawned. *Suddenly* something happened. Note these points:

The Sound

There was the "sound from heaven as of a rushing mighty wind." Wind is a symbol of the Holy Spirit. Present in gale force in the Upper Room, the wind represented the strength of the Divine Breath. God was breathing as His Spirit "filled all the house," and then the 120, and from there believers by the thousands.

The Sight

"Cloven tongues like as of fire . . . sat upon each of them." John the Baptist had said of Jesus, "He shall baptize you with the Holy Ghost, and with fire" (Matthew 3:11). One hundred and twenty obedient believers were seeing these words fulfilled. Myer Pearlman comments:

> The fact that the tongues of fire sat upon each of them was an indication of the beginning of a dispensation in which the Spirit of God was to be given not to the community as a whole, but to each member.

Fire is recognized throughout Scripture as a symbol of divine presence. It signifies cleansing, purifying, and sanctifying power.

The Utterance

"They were all filled with the Holy Ghost, and began to speak with other tongues, as the Spirit gave them utterance" (Acts 2:4).

The mysterious experience of magnifying God in languages prompted by the Spirit was the remarkable sign to the onlookers. The sound of wind may have created some attention but it was the speaking in other tongues that really attracted the crowd (2:6).

Why aren't the wind and fire evidences of the baptism of the Holy Spirit? The wind and the fire were emblems of the Holy Spirit, but the tongues were the first result of the coming of the Spirit. The former were the precursors of the actual receiving of the Spirit. Speaking in tongues is the one sign repeated in each instance when believers received the baptism in the Spirit.

The Dawn Wind

The dawn wind is the promise of morning. It breathes in the night the promise of light. Pentecost came with a wind. The Church was born. A new day dawned. The wind blew and it continues to blow. Its velocity has increased in recent years. Great things are taking place. The wind of the Spirit is God in action. The Holy Spirit is God at work.

Read the record of the work of the Spirit in Acts and you will feel you are in a factory, a workshop, where power is expressing itself. Activity is everywhere and things are getting done. Debate has been replaced by deeds. Movement and accomplishment are evident. Listen to the "dawn" wind and join in Spirit-directed activity.

2 The Dynamic Witness

Read: Acts 2:5 to 4:31

Nothing welds people together so soundly as a great common experience. In World War II the Nazis conquered Norway and used that base to launch attacks on the Allies' shipping lanes of the North Atlantic. The American army selected the 99th battalion and trained them for secret missions in Norway, a task that would be fraught with great danger. The men selected, Americans all, were of Norwegian descent; they became a tightly knit unit.

Thirty-five years later that unit still has an annual get-together. A preacher friend of mine is the current secretary of the group. Theirs was a great common experience.

Cemented Together

The deepest fellowship is born of things seen together and done together, and especially of things suffered together. The 120 gathered in the Upper Room in the strength of such a fellowship. They had suffered through the agonies surrounding their Master's trial and crucifixion. They had been knit together following His resurrection. A great expectation had drawn them together in the Upper Room. A common bond, a common life of prayer, a common expectancy, and now a great common experience at Pentecost.

The power at Pentecost transformed the disciples from little-known peasants into fiery prophets and from simple fishermen into fiery evangelists. This was the work of the mighty Holy Spirit.

The power at Pentecost was *personal*. Each one of the 120 had a personal experience. It wasn't theirs to the exclusion of everyone else, but theirs from the point of personal experience. "They were *all* filled" (Acts 2:4). The pattern was set for a normative experience for all members of the Church.

The power at Pentecost was *public*. While the experience was personal to each one, there was a sense in which it was not a "lone-ranger" matter. It was not something hidden in a corner. That which was poured on the 120 brought a multitude to hear and believe. The day began with 120 believers and ended with 3,000 converts. The Spirit came into thousands and the heartbeat of many became the heartthrob of one.

Above all, the power at Pentecost was a *Presence*. The promise given in the Upper Room prior to Gethsemane—"I will pray the Father, and he shall give you another Comforter" (John 14:16) was fulfilled. The Comforter had come. In His earthly ministry Jesus had been limited to one place at one time. The Holy Spirit became available to minister everywhere in the way that Jesus had only been able to do in personal contact. Now our Lord was not localized as He had been by His physical body; He is everywhere present by the Spirit. The Spirit does all Jesus could do by His bodily presence. He makes Christ real to us.

The ever-living Son of the Resurrection had become the ever-present Christ of Pentecost. The "one-accord" togetherness was the disciples' part; the filling with the Holy Spirit was God's part.

Obedience and Faith Bring Results

The 120 had been obedient. Now they were "endued with power from on high." They were transformed into flaming evangelists. The dynamic witness of the Church began at Pentecost and continues today. At times the flame has burned low and fervor has flagged, but whenever the Church has allowed the Spirit to move, a dynamic witness has taken place.

God Moves . . . Men Take Notice

The crowd that had assembled at the sound of the 120 worshiping and praising God in many tongues reacted in utter amazement. The astonishing thing was that they were speaking the praises of God in the languages of the nations and yet they were despised Galileans (Acts 2:7). The crowd was dumbfounded (v. 6); amazed and marveled (v. 7); and amazed and in doubt (v. 12). How could these simple Galileans speak in all these languages? Unbelievable! Little wonder they asked, "What meaneth this?" (v. 12).

Cynics, usually around wherever God works, were present to mock, "They're drunk, that's all" (v. 13). The world tends to attribute supernatural things to natural causes. Those who refuse to believe the works of God begin walking a path of rejection. This is illustrated in Acts. They began with mocking (2:13), then went on to raise questions (4:7), to threaten (4:17), to imprison (5:18), to do violence (5:40), and to murder (7:58-60).

Question of the Centuries

"What meaneth this?" has always been the cry of people as God has poured out His Spirit. This has been the cry of Bible students throughout the centuries as they have pondered the record in Acts. This has been the cry of thinking men ever since that eventful day in Jerusalem.

The cry of the centuries needs an answer. Do you know how simple people from the hills and seaside of Galilee could speak with the languages of ancient and cultured nations?

There Is an Answer

"What meaneth this?" Who would give the answer? None other than Peter; the disciple who had denied His Lord; but was now filled with the Spirit. Peter had an answer the rabbinical scholars did not have. His 3 years at the feet of the Master Teacher gave him a background of scriptural knowledge. Now he also possessed the experience.

True Preaching Centers on Christ

Read Peter's sermon and something will strike you. He used the occasion to present Jesus as Saviour, Lord, and Messiah. His presentation was so effective that 3,000 claimed Jesus as Saviour. Peter refuted the ridicule of the mockers (v. 15). What they had seen was not intoxication but a manifestation of the power of God. He identified the experience as a fulfillment of God's promise, with tongues being associated with the outpouring of the Spirit (vv. 16-18). Everything at Pentecost centered in Jesus. He had lived among the people and they had crucified Him, but God had raised Him from the dead. As the exalted Christ, He had sent this which they now saw and heard.

Peter left to others a more detailed explanation of the tongues phenomenon. The records concerning the manifestations at Jerusalem, Samaria, Damascus, Caesarea, and Ephesus are related for us by Luke in Acts. Paul outlines instruction concerning the exercise of the gift in public and private in his first letter to the Corinthians. Tongues were not given for evangelizing; Peter's sermon did that. Tongues are a sign of God's blessing and presence.

Preaching With Results

Peter's sermon brought visible results. First, there was *conviction*. The listeners were "pricked in their heart." (2:37). The preaching of the Word so affected them that they said, "What shall we do?"

Second, the preaching brought a *change*. Three thousand repented of their sins, believed on the Lord Jesus Christ, and were baptized (vv. 38, 41).

Third, a great *church* was established. The actual word *church* does not appear until Acts 5:11, but this was the church established at Pentecost. The components of a true church are mentioned: (1) teaching of doctrine; (2) fellowship in the Body; (3) worship through breaking of bread in the Lord's Supper; and (4) prayers (v. 42).

The power of the Lord manifest in that church was exhibited by: (1) reverential fear (v. 43); (2) sharing of material things (the believers voluntarily pooled their resources (vv. 44, 45). Apparently, this was a temporary practice for Paul later raised offerings for the saints at Jerusalem); (3) favor with all people (v. 47) (the picture is of a church in harmony and unity); and (4) daily growth (v. 47).

Putting It Simply

Acts 2 shows the Apostolic Church preserved its spiritual power by *teaching, fellowship, worship,* and *prayer.* Its spiritual power was manifested by *great influence* (v. 43), *great miracles* (v. 43), *great love* (vv. 44, 45), *great unity* (v. 46), *great joy* (vv. 46, 47), and *great growth* (v. 47).

The First Miracle

In Acts 3 we have the first recorded apostolic miracle. Peter and John were on their way to the temple for the time of afternoon prayer when they met a crippled man, lame from birth. The power Peter had used at Pentecost when a multitude had heard him preach and 3,000 were converted, was just as effective when applied to a crippled beggar.

The preaching of God's Word can stir the masses. But masses are made up of individuals, each of whom needs the Saviour. Peter and John had no hesitancy to help a solitary individual. From their 3 years of intensive training under Jesus they had learned their lesson well. Jesus dealt lovingly and patiently with people one by one, as well as with the thronging crowds.

What a challenging encounter! Suddenly these two Spirit-filled men found themselves in the presence of a deep human need. Here was a man lame from birth. What would these fellows endued with the power of the Holy Spirit do? The experience in the Upper Room had come to them spontaneously in a sense. This situation was different. Would the power work?

Putting It to the Test

Here they met: the beggar who picked the most profitable spot in Jerusalem to ply his trade (which was asking for money) and Peter and John. The apostles had come to pray; the cripple had come to beg.

The cripple's plight was desperate. Friends could move him from place to place, but that was all. No doubt he presented a revolting sight. Suffering and shame were his lot and he was looked on as a public nuisance.

Being over 40 years old, the cripple must have been at the Beautiful Gate often as Jesus came and went. Surely he must have heard reports of other cripples being made to walk. Well, that's conjecture. But this man lived through a remarkable era, one of miracles. And yet, his entire interest was alms. How like so many today. In this time of rich spiritual blessings, their interests are only material things.

Giving What You've Got

Peter said, "Look on us." Why this command? The beggar had to be aroused from his hopelessness. He wasn't looking for anything but money. And certainly he wasn't looking for healing; he had no faith.

"Silver and gold have I none; but such as I have give I thee" (3:6). Peter's words are immortal. He shared what he had. What he had was not money. Clothed with the power of the Spirit, Peter had something far more important than money. He had love and concern and more. "Such as I have . . ."— he didn't wait to act until his resources were doubled; what he had, he used. He knew the Christ who could do the impossible. And he believed!

Did the beggar think only of money? Or did he after all the bitter, frustrating years of pain and disgrace see something in the eyes of Peter and John? If he still continued to think only of money, his hopes were shattered.

It Works

Peter took him by the right hand. Through that hand raced the lifting, healing power of Jesus Christ. Peter *lifted* the man. Twisted, useless limbs surged with new life and strength. The man leaped up, stood, walked, and ran leaping, shouting, and praising God.

This incident lends itself easily to spiritualizing. But the simple, salient truth is that a man with a defect from birth, who regularly begged for a living,

18

was miraculously healed in the presence of many people.

Two Things Come Into Focus

First, there was a continuation of the ministry of Jesus, "of all that Jesus began . . . to do" (Acts 1:1). What He began to do in the days of His earthly sojourn, He continued to do after His ascension. *Second,* Jesus continues His ministry through His new body, the Church.

The story summarizes beautifully:

(1) *There was a beggar in abject poverty.* He was impoverished financially and physically and his morale had long since been shattered.

(2) *There was a preacher with ample provision.* He had that which would deliver the beggar from his disability rather than support him in his disability.

(3) *There was and is a Saviour with adequate power.* The healing was perfect. The Saviour is able to meet every need.

Thomas Aquinas is credited with the story about the money being counted in the church. Pope Innocent IV boasted, "The church can no longer say, 'Silver and gold have I none!' " To which Aquinas answered, "Neither can it say, 'Arise and walk.' " Such churches are pictured in Revelation 3:17, 18:

> Because thou sayest, I am rich, and increased with goods, and have need of nothing; and knowest not that thou are wretched, and miserable, and poor, and blind, and naked: I counsel thee to buy of me gold tried in the fire, that thou mayest be rich; and white raiment, that thou mayest be clothed, and that the shame of thy nakedness do not appear; and anoint thine eyes with eyesalve, that thou mayest see.

Peter's Second Sermon

Mighty works of the Holy Spirit are more effective testimony than any argument. The healed cripple, clinging to Peter and John, attracted a great deal of attention. As the crowd gathered, Peter was ready to preach. Seizing the initiative, as on the Day of Pentecost, he used the amazement of the crowd as an opportunity to witness.

As at Pentecost, Peter preached Christ crucified, risen, and exalted. He attributed the healing to the power of the living Christ (Acts 3:12-16). Preaching the truth without compromise, he exhorted the people to repentance. About 5,000 men believed (4:4).

The First Persecution

While Peter preached, the religious leaders, infuriated and troubled, imprisoned him and John. They were taken into custody, not because of the healing, but for preaching the doctrine of the resurrection (4:2). They were not questioned about their preaching, however, but about the healing of the cripple.

The question put to Peter—"By what power, or by what name, have ye done this?" (v. 7)—was exactly to Peter's liking. With a courtesy and boldness born of the Holy Spirit (v. 8), Peter made the great declaration: "Neither is there salvation in any other: for there is none other name under heaven given among men, whereby we must be saved" (v. 12).

The courage of Peter and John amazed the officials, especially when they saw they were common men, just the opposite of those distinguished by educational and social advantages. They recognized that Peter and John had been the very companions of Jesus himself. The hostile religious bigots were left confused and without argument. The witness of the apostles and the presence of the healed man robbed the Sanhedrin of their trusted weapons of defense. They scurried around for new weapons and fell back on an old one that's often used by a beaten antagonist—browbeating and threats.

From Court to Church

Having been threatened and commanded "not to speak at all nor teach in the name of Jesus" (4:18), Peter and John went to their fellow believers. Their report drove the church to prayer. God manifested himself by shaking the place where they prayed and again filling them all with the Holy Spirit.

3 The Church Under Fire

Read: Acts 4:32 to 8:1

For many years I lived in Minneapolis. From there comes the saga of a coat. The coat was owned and worn by Rangvald E. Nygaard of that city. Sometime in 1946 Mr. Nygaard donated it to the Lutheran World Relief clothing drive. With other clothing it was sent to a displaced persons' camp in Germany.

In 1950 a young Latvian, Juris Zankevics, was "resettled" and came to Minneapolis. He was assigned to one of the Lutheran Welfare Society's boarding homes—which happened to be the Nygaard home. A few days after he arrived there, Zankevics unpacked his trunk and hung some of his clothes out for an airing in the Nygaard backyard. Mrs. Nygaard saw a coat on the line, thought she recognized it, and called her husband. Sure enough, it was the one he had given to the clothing drive. The coat had come back—along with its new owner!

Cast Your Bread on the Waters

The saga of the coat brings to mind the verse: "Cast thy bread upon the waters: for thou shalt find it after many days" (Ecclesiastes 11:1). God has promised to bless the liberal person (Proverbs 11:24, 25).

After Pentecost a great impulse swept over these newly baptized people. They all wanted to help each other so they began to share what they had. "My" possessions became "our" possessions. These Spirit-filled disciples were surely free from the curse of covetousness. Their expression of generosity shows the wonderful sense of unity in the new life in Christ and the mutual dependence they shared as members of the infant Church.

What Does It Mean?

Graham Scroggie says of Acts 4:34-37:

This is a passage that may very easily be misinterpreted and misapplied, and indeed, has been. But there is nothing here comparable to modern communism. The reference to begin with, is not to the *State,* but to the *Church;* in the second place, the *social community* was based and sprang from *spiritual unity;* and once again, quite obviously the measure was exceptional and transitory, and disappeared within the apostolic age. But the spirit and the principle remain. All for each, and each for all, is the ideal of the Heavenly Commonwealth, for such is the Christian Church. Never, when the heart has been open, has the pocket been closed (Daily Notes, May 1929).

Living for Eternity—Practicing on Earth

Among those who contributed to the common fund was Barnabas, a native of sunny Cyprus. The island was known not only for its fertile valleys and prosperity, but also for its self-indulgent luxury.

Barnabas sold some property and gave the gross (not the net) profit to the apostles for their use in helping people. Apparently no big "to-do" was made over it; no special plaque was given him. But God marked it down for eternity. While others also were liberal, Barnabas is singled out in Scripture (4:36, 37).

The Heart . . . Billfold . . . Checkbook

Possessions, and our attitude toward them, are always a sure test of both character and consecration. There are no stingy Spirit-controlled Christians! When God reaches the heart He touches the billfold and the checkbook!

Have you ever noticed that when there has been a moving of the Spirit in your life or in your church the very first impulse is to share? You want to share your faith with someone else. Compassionate concern for others always marks the Spirit-filled Christian. When there are temporal needs, these are taken care of with the same love and concern as spiritual needs.

Don't Divorce

Riches are no menace if we don't divorce dollars from sense! But apparently some people have a bent along that line, for it seems that when it comes to giving they will stop at nothing!

Somewhere between the cradle and the funeral home there exists a strange bundle of excuses, who in the greatest kindness could be called a weak church member. Open that member's wallet and you will find last year's building-fund pledge card, a mission's faith promise, an empty church offering envelope, a check for a $125 car payment due next Tuesday, a baseball ticket stub, a 2-year-old church bulletin (Easter), a fishing license, one for hunting, and a list of New Year's resolutions (all broken).

Thank God this was not the picture of the Apostolic Church. Or how could they have evangelized their world?

God Deals With Bad Eggs

But there were some "bad eggs" in that church. One set was a husband-and-wife team—Ananias and Sapphira. The fellowship of the Jerusalem church—shared faith, shared concern, and even shared material possessions—was beautiful. But it was against this background of inspiring fellowship that the first serious threat came. Until then the threats had been external, but this was internal.

What's Your Motive?

The opening word of Acts 5 is significant, "But." Barnabas gave a gift motivated by love. Ananias and Sapphira gave also *but* with a different motive. Their sin was not keeping back a part of the price; their sin was lying. It was caused by greed, hypocrisy, and desire for praise.

The church had no law that everyone must sell all he had. The sharing of possessions was voluntary. Ananias and Sapphira planned to accomplish two things: (1) to earn a reputation for generosity; (2) but not to deprive themselves of cash.

God despises hypocrisy. Jesus denounced it when on earth (Matthew 23:23; Luke 11:42-44) and He has no use for it today. Hypocrisy is despicable. Avoid it like the plague.

I wonder, if every hypocrite should fall down dead on Sunday morning, how badly would churches be decimated? Not all Ananiases and Sapphiras are struck dead immediately, but God has shown what will be the eternal fate of all if they do not repent.

"Make all you can," cried John Wesley in one of his outdoor sermons. "Amen!" exclaimed a thrifty man. "In the second place," said Wesley, "save all you can." Again the man shouted, "Amen." "And in the third place I say," continued Wesley, "give all you can." "There now," moaned the disappointed fellow, "he's gone and spoilt it all."

Who Wants to Join a Church Where. . . ?

Ananias and Sapphira had lied not to men, but to God. The consequences were fatal—they were

25

struck dead! God had to show once and for all His attitude toward lying, deceit, and hypocrisy.

Their punishment had a sanctifying effect on that young church. They learned that God was holy, that He would not tolerate sin, and that all who professed to serve Him must do so with all their hearts. The believers were filled with wholesome fear.

Fear also came on the unbelievers. Those who may have wished to fall in with the popular tide of joining the church did not want to end up in the morgue. While they admired the church, they hesitated to join it unless they meant business. Who wants to join a church where hypocrites are struck dead?

Barnabas was a guiding light to the church; Ananias and Sapphira became beacons to warn against the shoals of disaster.

Great . . . Great . . . Great

Luke writes about the church having *great power, great grace,* and experiencing *great fear.* And when the Bible uses a word, it means exactly what it says. Because of the great manifestations by the Spirit in the church, "many signs and wonders" were wrought, multitudes of believers were added, and many healings (possibly hundreds) were performed, even to the extent that the sick tried to let the shadow of Peter fall on them as he passed by (5:12-15).

God is always at work in the affairs of men. Acts 5 illustrates three attitudes people take toward God's working: (1) hostility (vv. 17-28); (2) obedience (vv. 29-32); and (3) neutrality (vv. 33-39).

Some Are Hostile

The first apostolic miracle enraged the Jewish leaders. Then they became alarmed and infuriated to the point of desperation. Motivated by envy and jealousy, they threw the apostles in the common prison. "What audacity these ignorant Galileans have to threaten our prestige and ignore our orders"—that's what was in the minds of the religious leaders.

The apostles found themselves in prison, *but* the angel of the Lord delivered them (v. 19). Notice that "but." The priests thought they had a victory, "but"—that word is mighty when God uses it. "But God"—how many times Scripture records it.

Why did God deliver the apostles from prison but not from the beating they received the next day (v. 40)? They were delivered to "go, stand and speak in the temple to the people all the words of this life" (v. 20).

Some Obey

The apostles were rearrested and brought again before the Sanhedrin to be questioned. When asked why they had not ceased to teach in Jesus' name, they replied, "We ought to obey God rather than men" (v. 29). God first is the only rule for Christians. As Christians we are bound to obey the laws of the land (Romans 13:1-7) unless obedience to the laws would mean disobedience to God.

It is *possible* to obey man rather than God; this is wrong. It is *proper* to obey God rather than man; this is right. It is *practicable* to obey God and man; this is desirable. *Ought* is the important word.

Some Are Neutral

How many take the position of Gamaliel! Let's be neutral. "If this . . . be of men, it will come to nought: but if it be of God, ye cannot overthrow it; lest haply ye be found even to fight against God" (Acts 5:38, 39). While Peter and John had bleeding backs for their stand, Gamaliel remained neutral.

Gamaliel counseled the Sanhedrin to "let them alone." To this they agreed, but beat them first. Rather a strange way to let them alone. But "they ceased not to teach and preach Jesus Christ" and rejoiced "that they were counted worthy to suffer . . . for his name" (vv. 41, 42).

Another First

Firsts abounded in the Apostolic Church. Acts 6 records the first unrest, a "murmuring of the Grecians against the Hebrews" (v. 1). The infant church was subjected to the opposition of religious officials and tested within by attempted deceit. Now a new menace—dissension—threatened the unity of the church. Bitterness existed between the Hellenists (Grecian Jews) and the Palestinian Hebrews. It was all in the Jewish family as well as the church family. The Grecian Jews felt they were being discriminated against.

God gifted the Twelve with wisdom and they instructed the church by exercise of its own self-government to select seven men to care for material matters so the apostles could give themselves to "prayer, and to the ministry of the word" (v. 4).

Leaders Need Standards

The seven men chosen were not called *deacons*, but they filled a place of responsibility comparable to the office cited in 1 Timothy 3. Their qualifications were: (1) of honest report; (2) full of the Holy Spirit; and (3) full of wisdom. Stephen, one of the seven, was also "full of faith and power" (Acts 6:8).

What standards should be used in selecting leaders in a church? In the Apostolic Church they sought men of integrity and character. Nothing was mentioned about them being articulate or affluent. They were men from the ranks of the church. They sought men who met the standards set by the apostles. Their relationship with others was above reproach. Such men were found then and such is the standard for today. (See 1 Timothy 3:8-13.)

Stephen and Philip, two of the seven, gained attention as men extraordinarily used of the Lord. Stephen "did great wonders and miracles among the people" (Acts 6:8). Philip became well known as an effective evangelist (21:8).

Irresistible . . . Irrefutable . . . Invincible

The religious leaders were no match for Stephen as they sought to stop his ministry through lies by false witnesses (6:10-15). Stephen was arrested.

Stephen's arrest is the third recorded in Acts. First, it was Peter and John. Second, it was all the apostles. Third, it was Stephen. The first was followed by a warning, the second by a beating and a warning. In the third there was no warning or beating; Stephen was stoned to death.

Acts 7:1-53 is the record of Stephen's defense; it is the longest speech recorded in Acts. His defense is superb and merits detailed study. Little wonder that men like the brilliant young Saul were not able to withstand "the wisdom and the spirit by which he spake" (6:10).

The First Martyr

As Stephen concluded his defense by leveling an indictment against the Sanhedrin (7:51-53), the fury of his enemies was unleashed. They "ran upon him, . . . cast him out of the city, and stoned him" (vv. 57, 58). Mob violence took over, but Stephen, "full of the Holy Ghost . . . saw . . . Jesus standing on the right hand of God" (v. 55). With a prayer for forgiveness of his assailants, he passed triumphantly into the Lord's presence and became the first martyr. And, importantly, there was a young Pharisee from Tarsus named Saul standing nearby caring for the clothes of the executioners (v. 58). Someone has said the Church owes Paul to the prayers of Stephen.

Stephen, the *godly deacon* (6:1-7), became the *superb debater* (6-8-10) and the *capable defendant* (7:2-53), and concluded his ministry *triumphant in death* (7:54-60). He was *irresistible in debate, irrefutable in defense,* and *invincible in death.* Through the power of the Spirit, he exhibited unusual courage and faithfulness.

4   Faith Triumphant

Read: Acts 8:1 to 9:31

The greatest barrier to the expansion of the
Church is the silence of Christians. Witnessing for
Christ and breaking down the barriers of communi-
cation take many forms. Philip the evangelist witnessed before great crowds, bringing revival to the
city of Samaria, and then witnessed to a single
Ethiopian stranger in the desert.

A woman was found talking about Christ to a
wooden cigar-store Indian. When some friends, fearing she had become irrational, took her to task, she
replied, "I'd rather be a real Christian and talk salvation to a wooden Indian than a wooden Christian
who never talked about Jesus to anyone!" You think
she was crazy? If we have the good news and refuse
to tell others, we're crazier than she was!

Bitter Persecution

"Devout men carried Stephen to his burial, and
made great lamentation over him" (8:2).

Others reacted differently: "There was a great
persecution against the church which was at
Jerusalem" (8:1). The persecution was so bad the
believers were forced to flee. Driven out of
Jerusalem, the scattering must have been hard for
them. Never is it pleasant to leave the comforts of
home, friends, and a home church where love pre-

vails. They didn't choose to be scattered, any more than a family chooses to be evicted from their home. To be driven out must have seemed like a disaster.

Blessed Reaction

But the persecution worked against the persecutors. It was like a person kicking the embers of a fire in an attempt to put it out; the flames spread the greater. Every Christian became a torch to light a new fire where he went.

Let a farmer keep his seed in the bin and he grows no crop. Scatter the seed in the field and reap a harvest. Bottled up in Jerusalem, the Church would have withered and died. Scattered, it grew from Jerusalem to Samaria, to Asia, and as far off as Rome.

The persecuted went everywhere "preaching the word" (Acts 8:4). Their extremity became God's opportunity. Let us never forget that what happens to us is not nearly as important as what happens to God's cause in general.

Saul of Tarsus led the attack against the Church. While he seemed at first to be successful, his apparent success turned out to be a triumphant victory for the persecuted. Punch a pillow in the middle and it will fluff up on the ends.

A Second Stage

Acts 8 marks the second stage in the development of the Church. Up to this point, development had been under the direct ministry of the apostles in Jerusalem. The center of action shifted from the apostles to Stephen and Philip. Activity must reach the grass roots if the Church is to expand. And that is what happened as the disciples scattered (the apostles remained in Jerusalem) and the Church sprang up in far-off cities. In the process, Saul the persecutor was converted and became the apostle to the Gentiles.

Where the Rubber Hits the Road

What a lesson for us in our mobile society today. Because career and economy force them to do so, Americans are constantly on the move. Some who are Christians complain that it's hard to serve God where you have no family or friends. Apostolic Christians didn't want to move, but they were forced to flee for their lives and planted churches everywhere.

Powerful Preaching Brings Revival

Philip the layman went down to the city of Samaria. What an unlikely destination for a Jew unless he was Spirit-directed. The Jews wanted no dealings with the Samaritans (John 4:9). One of the "seven" appointed to "serve tables," Philip had a new avenue of service because of the persecution.

He went there and "preached Christ unto them" (Acts 8:5). Christ was his central theme and should be for all of us. The deacon-turned-evangelist found himself in a city-wide revival that brought "great joy in that city" (v. 8).

Word of the revival came to the apostles in Jerusalem. They sent Peter and John to Samaria. They recognized that the Samaritans had truly believed and obeyed the Word of God. They prayed for the Samaritans, laying hands on them, and they received the Holy Spirit (vv. 14-17). The Samaritans had received the Word, now they received the Holy Spirit in His fullness. Thus, the Samaritans were included in the Church. The apostles confirmed the revival and the Holy Spirit sanctioned and approved this step of expansion.

Several important truths concerning the person and work of the Holy Spirit are revealed in the Samaritan revival: (1) Those converted were urged to pray that they might receive the Holy Spirit (v. 15) (see also Luke 11:13; Acts 9:17, 18; 19:1-7; 1 Corinthians 12:30; 14:1); (2) This experience took place subsequent to the new birth; and (3) The experience is for all believers (Acts 8:14-17).

There's Always a Counterfeit

Either through occult power or trickery, Simon the sorcerer capitalized on the gullibility of the masses. He was baptized and "wondered, beholding the miracles and signs" (8:13).

When Simon saw Peter and John lay their hands on the Samaritans he noted a spectacular happening. He had seen many miracles accompany Philip's ministry. This was something different that intrigued him. Many New Testament scholars, including Adam Clarke and Matthew Henry, believe the Samaritans spoke in tongues as they received the Holy Spirit.

Simon wanted this power. He offered to buy it, bringing a new word into the vocabulary of the Church—*simony*. The two Simons faced each other. Simon Magus was hardly prepared for the denunciation Simon Peter gave him: "Thy money perish with thee. . . . Thy heart is not right. . . . Repent" (vv. 20-23).

Why Leave a Revival?

Having won crowds in Samaria, Philip now had marching orders to the desert (8:26). Odd instructions indeed! But how wonderful to be at the disposal of God. Centuries before, Abraham knew *why* God sent him out but not *where*. Philip knew *where* but not *why*.

How clearly the message comes to us in all of these incidents. The gospel is to be either *given away* or *given up*. If it is what we say it is we must give it away. If it is not, we must give it up. The good news is a commodity that can't be cornered, frozen, or stockpiled. We possess it as we pass it on and we retain it as we share it.

On the Gaza road Philip found an Ethiopian. Here was a preacher chosen by the Holy Spirit, an audience chosen by the Spirit, a place chosen by the Spirit, and a text chosen by the Spirit. The Ethiopian was reading Isaiah 53, a perfect text. The Spirit led Philip in a beautiful series of incidents resulting in the conversion of the man as Philip "preached unto him Jesus" (8:35). Philip must have not only preached repentance, but also water baptism, for the eunuch requested to be baptized right along the road. The eunuch went on his way rejoicing in his newfound faith and Philip was caught away (v. 39).

The Ethiopian became the first recorded Gentile convert. The conversion of this influential man may have been God's way of getting the gospel into Africa. In one sense there is the possibility that the effects of this ministry may have been as effective as the revival in Samaria.

A Fiendish Persecutor

Chapter 9 brings a turning point in the Book of Acts. A man is introduced who dominates the narrative from this point on.

This man, Saul (later to be known as the apostle Paul), entered the picture at the stoning of Stephen. Tireless, relentless, and without pity, he flung himself into the task of attempting to stamp out Christians and Christianity. He was one of the strict "fundamentalists" of his day and he separated himself from all the Pharisees considered evil. Sincerity consumed him as he went about his "threatenings and slaughter," believing he was doing right to wipe out this heretical sect.

A Sudden Stop

Saul's reign of terror came to an abrupt halt, however, when confronted with a dazzling heavenly light and the person of Christ. Envision the startling scene. The flashing light from heaven engulfing him, the overwhelming view of the Saviour, the authoritative yet gentle voice from Glory—and all the while the fiery fanatic lying in the dust on the Damascus road. Recognition of the Almighty came quickly: "Who art thou, Lord? . . . Lord, what wilt thou have me to do?" (9:5, 6).

Saul's conversion was dramatic, swift, and complete. Blinded, totally awed, and subdued he went without food and drink for 3 days. At this point the ministry of a *middleman* entered the scene. That man was Ananias, of whom nothing is previously recorded and who disappears from the record almost as soon as he appears. After being assured by the Lord that Paul was a changed man, Ananias immediately went to Judas' house on Straight Street to minister to this newborn child of God. As he laid his hands on him and prayed, Saul received his sight. Then he was baptized. His physical need for food, his filling with the Spirit, and his instruction in the things of the Lord took place.

As a mighty transatlantic liner needs a tugboat to start it out of the harbor, and as a spaceship needs an auxiliary blast to launch it into space, Paul was launched into his mighty ministry by faithful men of less renown who stood by him.

A Man Transformed

The conversion of Saul stands out as one of the

most astounding miracles of history. For Saul it was a complete about-face. To think the Church's most violent enemy would turn around and seek the help of those he had threatened to kill! But beyond that was the complete transformation of Saul's whole being. Christ took possession of his mind, his emotions, his will, his desires, and his very body. Saul illustrated this later when he wrote: "If any man be in Christ, he is a new creature: old things are passed away; behold, all things are become new" (2 Corinthians 5:17).

This story of Saul's arrest, or apprehension, becomes even more significant as we read what he wrote nearly 30 years later: "Not as though I had already attained, . . . but I follow after, if that I may *apprehend* that for which also I am *apprehended* of Christ Jesus" (Philippians 3:12).

The conversion of Saul led to some beautiful incidents in the life of the young Church. Ananias greeted this archenemy of the Church with the heartwarming greeting, "Brother Saul" (Acts 9:17). The scenes in the house of Judas are a window through which we can see the Church acting—the convert praying, the right hand of fellowship extended to welcome a former enemy as a brother, and the care given that brother, including his bodily needs, as a token of Christian love and grace. Truly they welcomed this one who was to be "a chosen vessel" (v. 15) in love without a trace of bitterness, animosity, or jealousy.

On Fire for God

The new believer lost no time but began witnessing, "Straightway he preached Christ" (v. 20). As could be expected, the persecutor soon became the persecuted. He became the object of a plot to murder him, but he made a thrilling escape (v. 25; 2 Corinthians 11:32, 33). He made his way to Jerusalem but the church was hesitant to receive him because of his past reputation. How beautiful was the action of another *middleman*. Barnabas came to his aid and vouched for him (Acts 9:27).

Boldly proclaiming Christ in Jerusalem, his life again became endangered. The brethren arranged for him to go to Caesarea, from where he went to his home city of Tarsus, and remained there for some time (vv. 29, 30).

The dramatic conversion of Saul has troubled many agnostics. One such, Lord George Lyttleton, proposed to show it would be impossible for a man like Saul to have such a change of direction in his life.

Lyttleton plunged into his task with enthusiasm. His research was published in a book titled *Observations on the Conversion and Apostleship of St. Paul.* His conclusion is most interesting: "Paul's conversion and apostleship alone, duly considered, are a demonstration sufficient to prove Christianity to be a divine revelation."

And Lyttleton himself became converted to Christ!

5 Beyond Church Walls

Read: Acts 9:32 to 12:25

Before turning his attention almost exclusively to Paul's ministry and missionary journeys, Luke returns his narrative to the ministry of Peter. The last 12 verses of Acts 9 record Peter's visit to Lydda and Joppa and the two miracles God performed through him in those two cities.

Miracles were part and parcel of the gospel. Pompey boasted that with one stamp of his foot he could rouse all Italy to arms. But God by one word of His mouth can summon the inhabitants of heaven and earth to do His will. The basic difference between physical and spiritual power is that men use and abuse physical power but spiritual power uses men.

And surely it was spiritual power that used Peter to perform miracles. Not for all the wealth of the world could anyone do what he accomplished at Lydda and Joppa except through the power of the Holy Spirit in Jesus' name.

Aeneas had been sick for 8 years. Rather discouraging, wasn't it? Many of us would have come to the conclusion that it wasn't God's will to heal this man who apparently was one of the "saints" in Lydda. Obviously, it was a sad and hopeless case.

A Short Prayer Will Reach the Throne
If You Don't Live Too Far Away

I am struck with the brevity of Peter's prayer. In fact, Peter simply made a declaration, "Aeneas, Jesus Christ maketh thee whole: arise, and make thy bed" (v. 34). How similar to our Lord's commands when He walked among men in need. While this was a command of bold, confident faith, there is no question but what it was born out of a walk in the Spirit.

Two women on boarding a jet plane requested the pilot to not fly faster than sound for "we want to talk." We are prone to talk too much. Even when we pray we do more talking than listening. As M. P. Horban points out: "We've taken the grand word of Samuel, 'Speak; for thy servant heareth' (1 Samuel 3:10), and we have turned it around to say, 'Listen, Lord; for thy servant speaketh.'"

Peter was in touch with the Great Healer. His words, "Jesus Christ maketh thee whole," were a confident declaration of Christ's ability and the fact that Jesus was at work in the Church and that the apostle was but His instrument.

The results of the healing of Aeneas paralleled those of the lame man at the Beautiful Gate. The miracle proved to be the opening wedge for evangelism. Many turned to the Lord.

Time for a Funeral, but . . .

During this time the church at Joppa, a few miles northwest of Lydda, suffered a great loss. The saintly Dorcas, much loved for her "good works and almsdeeds *which she did,*" died. Her faith Godward resulted in her works manward. She was both devout and dedicated to the needs of others. Her fingers and her needle were constantly and sacrificially busy.

But Dorcas became ill and died. Why does God

permit things to happen that result in dismay and tears? The sequel provides the answer in this case. While the life of Dorcas was influential to bless many, her death—and subsequent resurrection—brought great glory to God and great inspiration and blessing to people. The news of the miracle spread throughout "all Joppa; and many believed in the Lord" (v. 42).

Why a Miracle?

Note some other lessons from this incident. *First,* the purpose of apostolic miracles. There are three words in the New Testament for miracles—*wonders, signs,* and *mighty deeds.* The *wonder* suggests the effect on the witness; the *sign* connects it with the accompanying testimony; and the *mighty deed* denotes the power entailed in its achievement. Mighty works authenticated the ministry of Jesus, and God wants to do the same today. The Great Commission concludes with the statement that the Lord was "working with them, and confirming the word with signs following" (Mark 16:20). The message was confirmed by the miracle (Hebrews 2:3, 4).

A second lesson is the illustration of the truth that God does wonderful things for people who may not be great in name, position, or rank. True, Dorcas was known for her good deeds in Joppa, but her life was basically obscure and her ministry was quiet. She loved God, she loved people, and she consecrated her needle. Her ambition was to serve and to do good.

Another lesson I wish to emphasize is the blessing of the Spirit-directed life. Think how the Spirit directed Peter in various ways. He went to Samaria at the request of the apostles. He came to Lydda in the course of his evangelistic ministry, to Joppa by the

41

urging of the saints there, and to Caesarea (Acts 10) by a vision and the direct command of God.

God Told Me

Have you noted people who speak so freely of allegedly being told by God to do something, and yet see how their lives and follow-up indicate great contradictions? The secret of the leading of the Spirit is in yieldedness to His control.

A Turning Point

Acts 10 records one of the great turning points in the history of the Apostolic Church. The Church was at first only a Jewish sect. Jewish pride and prejudice and Gentile ignorance placed almost insurmountable barriers to the spread of the gospel. Was the gospel for the Jew or was it to reach the world? Was the Gentile to come under Jewish restrictions? Could the Gentile come directly into the Church through faith or must he come through Judaism?

A Crack Opens

Prior to the outpouring of the Spirit in Caesarea (as recorded in this chapter), God had poured out the Spirit on the Day of Pentecost and also in Samaria. Those who received at Pentecost were either Jews or proselytes to the Jewish faith from among the Gentiles. The Samaritans were of mixed blood, being part Jewish and part Gentile. Their Jewish forebears had intermarried with the nations brought in by the Babylonians. The outpouring in Samaria was a crack in the wall of prejudice.

But there was still no place in the church for a Gentile who had not become a full proselyte and followed the traditional Jewish way of life with its regulations regarding kosher foods and other rites of Judaism. Limited to Jews, Samaritans, and proselytes, the church was by no means fulfilling the Great Commission. Nor was the church ready for the apostle Paul, and possibly he wasn't ready for his assignment (Acts 9:15).

God did, however, as always, have someone for the task. Peter, a member of the Lord's inner circle, was chosen. The job was big, but Peter knew the voice of the Spirit and became obedient.

God Works at Both Ends

While God was dealing with Peter in a supernatural way, he was also dealing with a devout Roman. God laid one hand on Peter the Jew and the other on Cornelius the Italian army officer, bringing the two together for the big breakthrough. There are similarities in this experience to that of Ananias and Paul (Acts 9).

Cornelius was a seeker after the things of God. He wanted something he hadn't found. His burden led him to pray. In response to his prayer, God sent an angel, not to preach the gospel to him, but to tell him where he could get a preacher.

While the Holy Spirit was preparing Cornelius, He was also preparing the Jewish preacher. Apparently some of Peter's hang-ups were being dissipated for he was a houseguest of Simon the Tanner. Simon's was a defiling occupation among the Jews.

One day while awaiting a meal, Peter went up on the housetop to pray. As he prayed he had an amazing vision of a sheet let down from heaven with unclean animals on it. He was told to arise, kill, and eat, but he refused. Three times this happened and then the sheet was taken back up into heaven. It could hardly be unclean if it was received into heaven. While this was happening the messengers dispatched by Cornelius to bring Peter to Caesarea arrived.

Through this experience Peter came to the conclusion that: (1) God wanted the Gentiles in the Church (10:17-20); (2) there is no difference in the Church Age between Jew and Gentile (v. 28); (3) fellowship, even in each other's homes, was God's will for Jewish and Gentile believers (10:27; 11:2, 3); and (4) the Mosaic law was abrogated as a barrier between Jew and Gentile (15:1, 10, 11, 24, 28, 29).

A New Preaching Experience

Shortly Peter found himself with his party of six preaching to the family and near friends of Cornelius. He opened his sermon with a profound truth—"God is no respecter of persons" (10:34). From there he proceeded to preach Christ crucified and risen, showing the practical meaning of it all was to bring salvation to all who "through his name . . . [believe] in him" (10:43). At this point Peter experienced a divine interruption. Cornelius and his household were saved and filled with the Holy Spirit. How did Peter know? "For they heard them speak with tongues, and magnify God" (10:46). Immediately the new converts were also baptized in water. This outpouring signaled the birth of the Gentile church.

The report of the happenings in Caesarea reached Jerusalem and became a matter of contention. Peter arrived in town and was called to report on matters. Instead of appealing to his apostolic authority or asserting his position, Peter wisely confined himself to telling what God had done. Fortunately, he had the witness of the six brethren who had been with him (11:12).

An Example Is Worth a Thousand Arguments

Peter's simple, unadorned account followed this line of reasoning: (1) God revealed to him the fallacy of rejecting God's work among Gentiles. Tradition said no; but God said yes (11:5-10). (2) External providence supported internal promptings (vv. 11-14). (3) God confirmed His Word and the Gentiles received the same experience the 120 had received at Pentecost (vv. 15-17). How significant are his words: "What was I, that I could withstand God?"

Three "Conversions"

The incidents surrounding the Cornelius experience can be summarized as three *conversions* (using the word in a wider sense than that related to the salvation of sinners). The first conversion, however, was that of salvation; Cornelius and his household received Christ as Saviour.

The second "conversion" was that of Peter. Somewhat baffled, he squirmed under the impact of the vision received on the housetop. At first he refused to obey God's strange command. But as the Spirit dealt with him, he saw God's direction. With boldness he stepped across the ethnic boundary to become the first missionary to the Gentiles. It is to Peter's credit that he recognized that if God intended to save Gentiles, he wanted to be ready to be His instrument to accomplish His purpose.

The third "conversion" was that of the church. The mother church shared Peter's exclusiveness. The record indicates, however, that the Jerusalem church received Peter's testimony with: (1) agreement—"they held their peace"; (2) appreciation—they "glorified God"; and (3) acceptance—"then hath God also to the Gentiles granted repentance unto life" (11:18).

Redemption is to be worldwide in its outreach. Racial barriers are to be nonexistent. Religious pride and bigotry are rebuked. Gentiles are to be equal in privilege and opportunity with the Jews.

The Kindly Investigator

The mother church had continuing problems accepting this broadening ministry. Word reached them of the revival in Antioch where the message was being preached to the Greeks. The church delegated the kindly Barnabas to investigate the situation and to ascertain the results.

Barnabas found a wonderful revival with nothing that needed correction, and remained to minister and saw many added to the Lord. Apparently he felt the need for help, so he made his way to Tarsus to enlist the services of Saul. These two friends remained for a joint Bible-teaching, pastoral ministry for a year in this city where the believers were first called Christians (11:26).

How significant that when Agabus prophesied a coming drought, the Antioch church sent relief by the hands of Saul and Barnabas to the believers in Judea (vv. 28-30). The grace of God was truly breaking the barriers of prejudice.

A Conniving Politician

About this time Herod stirred up persecution (Acts 12). He had James the brother of John killed, making James the first apostle to earn the martyr's crown. Being a keen politician, Herod saw the political expediency of attempting to destroy Christianity. His next target was Peter. Peter was arrested and held in prison for a week. Closely guarded by 16 Roman soldiers, he was to be executed after 7 days of the Passover.

But Prayer

The one resource available to the church as it was overwhelmed by this sudden outburst of ferocious persecution was prayer. *"But prayer* was made *without ceasing* of the church unto God for him" (12:5). What a resource!

The night before his execution Peter was sleeping soundly (could you do so?) when another miracle took place. God sent His angel and delivered him. When Peter arrived at the house where the church was in prayer, they were slow to believe that God had answered their prayer. Even Rhoda, the maid who met Peter at the door, was called crazy. How strange, and yet how much like us today!

Herod had the 16 soldiers court-martialed and put to death. Like so many before him and after him, he thought of himself more highly than he ought to have. God's judgment fell on him and he died an ignoble death (12:23).

"But the word of God grew and multiplied" (v. 24). The word *but* occurs again. On the one hand was the horrible death of Herod, the persecutor. On the other hand was the growth of the Church. Men may come and men may go, but God's church marches on.

Each new wave of opposition served only to propagate the gospel further. The Church was ravaged by 10 bloody persecutions under the pagan Roman emperors. After each had spent itself, Christianity was only the stronger.

Throughout the centuries the testimony of growth in the face of persecution has been recorded. Many are the stories that can be told from behind the iron and bamboo curtains and elsewhere in this century.

6 Launching Into New Territories

Read: Acts 13 and 14

Michael Faraday, the renowned scientist, as a boy sold newspapers. One day while waiting for his papers in front of the iron gates of the newspaper office, he put his arms and head through the bars. Already scientifically inclined, he began to analyze the situation. With his arms and head on one side of the gate and his heart and body on the other side, on which side was the real Michael Faraday?

He says that at this point someone opened the gate and nearly jerked his head off. He quickly learned there is nothing to be gained and plenty to lose by being on both sides at the same time! You've got to take your stand. The price paid is far less than the loss that comes to those seeking neutrality.

No Chance to Ride the Fence

Acts 13 relates several incidents: God's call to Barnabas and Saul, the first missionary journey, Satan's opposition, Paul's sermon in Antioch of Pisidia, more opposition, and a turn to ministry to the Gentiles.

Saul (let's begin calling him Paul) and Barnabas faced a slowly rising tide of opposition. There was no place for neutrality, no chance to ride the fence. The narrative reminds us of the wagon trains starting West. They were driving into strange country; invading "Gentile country" for the first time. From here on in Acts, Paul becomes the central, dominating figure.

Sticking Your Neck Out

When he was president of Harvard, Dr. James B. Conant kept a strange object on his desk—the model of a turtle. Under the turtle was a carved inscription: "Consider the turtle. He makes progress only when he sticks his neck out."

Paul stuck his neck out: he called everything but the knowledge and the will of God refuse. He set his face toward the Gentile world. Great things would happen. Churches would be planted. Congregations would be organized and taught. The gospel would reach distant cities and eventually the great champion would pay the supreme sacrifice in Rome.

From Little Acorns . . .

What a long way the Church had come from her small beginning in the Upper Room. Persecution had scattered the Christians everywhere carrying the good news. Judea and Samaria had been reached according to the divine plan. The groundwork had been laid for carrying the message to the uttermost parts. Peter had been convinced of the universality of the gospel. A center of Gentile evangelism had been established at Antioch in Syria, led by Barnabas who had summoned Paul to be his helper. In a sense the initiative for world evangelism would be invested in these two men of God, both Jews, with the backing of a Gentile church.

This bit of Church history presents a composite picture that is worthy of a distinct place in the memory of modern Christians. Behind the authoritative ministry of Paul and his yokefellow Barnabas was a church that prayed.

Historic Prayer Meeting

Five ministers—prophets and teachers—in the Antioch church were ministering to the Lord. This is a much neglected part of our lives. They waited before God in worship, extolling Him. Ministering to Him is not so much praising Him for what He has done and will do, but for who He is. These men were "blessing" the Lord and fasting and praying. This unhurried and unregimented action is never crowded; too few participate. Out of their waiting on God came the clear direction to ordain Paul and Barnabas as apostolic oracles for an apostolic operation.

There have been many historic prayer meetings in Church history. None can rival in importance the prayer meeting held in the Antioch assembly in the year A.D. 46 or 47 and recorded so simply and briefly in Acts 13:1-3. World missions, while in the heart of God from eternity, began its realization as the men ministered, prayed, and fasted together.

The Scriptures indicate a twofold sending of this first missionary team. They were sent by the church with laying on of hands (13:3) and sent by the Holy Spirit (13:4). The inference seems clear that God had spoken previously to Paul and Barnabas in a personal way, and now He was confirming that call.

Heading Out

Thus from Antioch, the center of Christian activity, Paul embarked on the first of his three missionary journeys. Each began there and ended there, except the last which ended with his arrest in Jerusalem. Traveling with him were Barnabas and

John Mark, a relative of Barnabas. What a modest beginning for world missions—two men and a youth!

The first stop on the journey was Cyprus, the island home of Barnabas. The estate that Barnabas, the "son of consolation," had sold to meet the needs of the saints in the Jerusalem church was located there.

Becoming Second Fiddle

At Paphos a significant change took place. Saul, from now on called Paul (13:9), took the leadership. Saul was his Hebrew name (a namesake of King Saul who was also of the tribe of Benjamin); Paul was his Roman name (he was a Roman by birth).

How beautiful was the spirit and attitude of Barnabas. He had befriended Paul as a new convert and secured for him the hand of fellowship in the Jerusalem church. Recognizing his ability as a minister, Barnabas had invited Paul to join him in ministry in the Antioch church. Many would have insisted on maintaining the place of prominence because of seniority—the first to walk through the door, the prominent seat, the key place on the program. Not so with the "son of consolation." Never was there a trace of envy, jealousy, or rancor; the greathearted, kindly, benevolent Barnabas put the will of God first and accepted in Christian grace the place God gave him. He was truly a "good man." His later disagreement with Paul doesn't negate this.

Look Out Workers of Witchcraft!

At Paphos, Sergius Paulus, the highest Roman officer in Cyprus, had a desire to hear the gospel. But whenever God begins to work, opposition comes from the enemy. Elymas, a sorcerer who was employed as magician to Sergius Paulus, was the devil's tool to oppose the work. Elymas had a good thing going and he was unwilling to give up his lucrative grip on the community without a fight. But Paul possessed that extra dimension, the power of the Spirit. By the Spirit Paul discerned the man, by the Spirit he rebuked the man, and by the Spirit he pronounced judgment. Elymas was to become blind for a period of time. The miracle of judgment took place immediately. The Roman ruler believed and the preaching of the Word was confirmed (13:6-12).

After their tour of Cyprus, the missionary team sailed north to Perga on the south shore of Asia Minor, and set out across the Taurus Mountains into Galatia and the city of Antioch (in Pisidia). The route passed through rugged mountains and across roaring rivers. Robbers infested the region. Paul may have referred to this trip when he wrote, "in perils of waters, . . . of robbers, . . . in the wilderness" (2 Corinthians 11:26). This last difficult trek was made without John Mark who left them (Acts 13:13), a decision that would later have repercussions.

Another First

Attention focuses on Antioch. Paul's custom as he visited various cities was to preach first in the Jewish synagogue; a courtesy allowed visiting teachers. Here at Antioch we have his first recorded sermon.

Paul's powerful sermon is an example of good preaching (13:16-41). Below is an outline of it:

    I. Review of Israel's history (13:16-23)
       A. Israel in Egypt (v. 17). God chose them, made them great, and led them out.
       B. Israel in the wilderness (v. 18). God bore with them.
       C. Israel enters Canaan (v. 19). Emphasis is on God, not on leaders.
       D. Israel under the judges (v. 20). Paul presents the positive picture of God's provision.
       E. Israel under Saul (v. 21).
       F. Israel under David (v. 22).

G. Israel under David's posterity (v. 23). Paul establishes Old Testament credentials for David's greater Son. Paul is leading up to its climax with the death and resurrection of Jesus.

II. Review of the life of Christ (13:26-31)
   A. Salvation is now available (v. 26).
   B. Jesus was condemned (v. 27).
   C. Jesus was killed and buried (vv. 28, 29).
   D. God raised Him from the dead (v. 30).
   E. Jesus appeared to witnesses (v. 31).

III. The appeal (13:32-41)
   A. Sharp focus on Jesus (vv. 32-39).
   B. Beware of rejecting the Saviour (vv. 40, 41).

The sermon resulted in many turning to Christ and the impact was such that "almost the whole city" came "together to hear the word of God" on the next Sabbath (v. 44).

Popularity . . . Persecution
A Slight Swing of the Pendulum

Paul and Barnabas met both popularity and persecution, and they never were very far apart. They met both acceptance and rejection in Cyprus (13:7, 8), and the same occurred in Antioch. Nearly the whole town turned out to hear the gospel. But the Jewish reaction was monotonously negative. They became so jealous that they contradicted the message and blasphemed (v. 45). They thought they had a special claim on God and couldn't tolerate the openness to the Gentiles. How deep-seated and devastating prejudice can be!

The opposition of the Jews stirred Paul and Barnabas to holy boldness and they made a significant declaration: "We turn to the Gentiles" (13:46). And here we have another great turning point in Church history.

Splitting a City

Paul and Barnabas "shook off the dust of their

feet" and went on to Iconium. Although the Jews at Antioch bitterly persecuted them, they did not fail to preach to the Jews (14:1). Again God blessed their ministry: "A great multitude both of the Jews and also of the Greeks believed." Imagine the effectiveness of the gospel. It was no small movement that fairly split a city in two in a matter of weeks (14:4). To divide a village, yes; to split a city, that's impact!

An attempt was made to stone the missionaries. Paul, who once persecuted the Christians, was now being persecuted by his own people. But the planned stoning must have hurt his heart even more than it would have his body. They fled to Lystra. And what did they do? Go into hiding? Give up? No. "There they preached the gospel" (14:7).

Sent to Win Souls, Not Fame

A remarkable response took place. Paul came upon a cripple, lame from birth. With keen spiritual insight, Paul recognized that the man had faith. He commanded him, "Stand. . . . And he leaped and walked" (14:10).

To the heathen population of Lystra there could be only one explanation: "The gods are come down to us in the likeness of men" (v. 11). The people in wild enthusiasm prepared to worship them. Here was peril. Prosperity of any kind can be dangerous, but praise is the most subtle and deceitful. A sincere expression of praise is appreciated, but beware of becoming a victim of flattery. Few can resist it, much to their detriment.

Pride Brings Problems

Pride is at the heart of personal, church, national, and international problems. It may be pride of race, of face, of place, and even of grace.

Paul and Barnabas left an excellent example. The

people were determined to worship them; they were determined the people should not. With all that the apostles could say, "Scarce restrained they the people, that they had not done ‿acrifice unto them" (v. 18). A member of one of America's wealthiest churches was asked why she liked that particular church. Her reply: "It isn't the church; it's the pastor. He always puts God first and himself last." That was true of the greatest apostle, Paul.

Glory Today . . . Gone Tomorrow

How fickle people are. Paul's enemies came from Antioch and Iconium and stirred up the Lystrans to stone Paul and leave him for dead outside the city. Paul looked back on his experiences here as both his most triumphant and most bitter. We can read about them in his farewell letter to Timothy:

> But thou hast fully known my doctrine, manner of life, purpose, faith, long-suffering, charity, patience, persecutions, afflictions, which came unto me at Antioch, at Iconium, at Lystra; what persecutions I endured: but out of them all the Lord delivered me (2 Timothy 3:10, 11).

And yet Paul never wavered in his love for his own people. He would gladly have given everything, including becoming "accursed from Christ" to see them saved (Romans 9:3).

Down but Not Done

Paul lay on the ground outside Lystra apparently dead. But "the disciples stood round about him," no doubt praying in faith. God raised him up and Paul went right back to preaching.

"And when they had preached the gospel . . ." (14:21). Few phrases are more significant. The cataclysmic changes following the preaching of the gospel are more effective, startling, and beneficial than those caused by any other force in the world.

It Takes Courage

From Derbe Paul and Barnabas could easily have reached home by continuing eastward through the great pass of the Taurus Mountains, but they chose to go back the way they had come. They retraced their steps from Derbe through Lystra, Iconium, Antioch in Pisidia, Pamphylia, Perga, and into Attalia. This took courage because it meant they would face enemies from whom they had recently fled. They did this to strengthen the young churches in the faith and to provide for their future growth.

The "father" hearts of Paul and Barnabas reached out to their spiritual children. There was every probability that the Christians were already suffering for their faith since the apostles expressly spoke of the value of tribulation (14:22). Persecution and suffering was the way of life for those early Christians.

The missionaries appointed elders in each church to direct and lead the assemblies. Imagine the moving experiences as the missionaries fasted and prayed with their converts, commending them to the Lord. They didn't know if they would ever see each other again.

Featured Speakers

Finally they arrived in Antioch in Syria from where they had started. The first missionary journey was now history. They had been gone for nearly 2 years and had traveled 1,400 miles. New churches had been started wherever they went. New workers, such as Timothy and Gaius, who were to become leaders, had been thrust forth into the ministry of the gospel. A full report of how God "had opened the door of faith unto the Gentiles" (14:27) was shared with the church that had sent them and supported them. They were the "featured speakers" at a great missionary convention. Paul and Barnabas remained in Antioch for a long period of ministry.

7   The Jerusalem Crisis

Read: Acts 15:1-35

The pastor of a little missionary outpost in the jungle set up a temporary church. His pulpit was an old box he had picked up on the street. When he got up to preach his first sermon he was startled to discover two words stenciled in black on the side of the box: "Danger! Explosives!"

The Apostolic Church ran into trouble because its stock in trade was an explosive gospel. Planting the gospel was like planting a time bomb; sooner or later, it was bound to go off.

Paul delighted in the dynamite of the gospel. He didn't care much for a church that wasn't loaded with dynamite and forever making people fear an explosion into action.

The Church was born in a divided world. Its ministry was to a divided world. Inevitably the Church was made up of people who brought the divisions and prejudices of the contemporary scene with them.

Exploding . . . Shattering . . . Blasting

But the great premise of the gospel was that God is no respecter of persons. The gospel not only exploded on the heathen; its message of grace also shattered Jewish tradition. Prejudice was blasted to smithereens.

Chapter 15 is one of the crucial chapters of Acts because it records the great Jerusalem conference. The big issue was the gospel versus legalism. The matter of free grace was in direct conflict with religious traditionalism. The Judaizers complained that the Gentiles could not be accepted into the church as persons. Who were the Judaizers? They were Jewish Christians who felt the Gentiles should be circumcised and follow the law of Moses before they could be accepted into the Christian fellowship.

Not All Bad, but . . .

Differences are not always bad; they are the mark of freedom. The big concern is what we do with our differences and what they do to us. Try living with a fellow who is never wrong! It's like the fellow who said about another, "He's the most consistent person I've ever met. He's always right."

The Antioch church recognized the seriousness of this debate. The doctrine of the Judaizers threatened the very life of the church which was predominantly Gentile in nature. Unless they came under Mosaic law, their acceptance in divine favor was incomplete (15:1)—according to the Judaizers.

Why Jerusalem?

Paul chose not to exercise his apostolic authority in Antioch. This issue would have to be settled in Jerusalem—where it all began. The original apostles (Paul became an apostle later than the Twelve) had their seat there. Jerusalem must be the place where the legalism yoke would be broken and the issue of grace and law be settled once and for all.

A delegation led by Paul and Barnabas was selected and sent to Jerusalem to confer with the apostles and elders there about the issue. En route they reported to the churches in Phoenicia and

Samaria on the conversion of the Gentiles. These churches rejoiced that the door had been opened to the Gentiles.

The First General Council

The apostles and elders welcomed the brethren and held an open meeting—a General Council, if you please—to give a hearing on the issue. It is believed by many that Paul's letter to the Galatians (2:1-10) refers to the matters discussed on this momentous occasion.

No Place for Peace at Any Price

Possibly after a cursory reading of Acts 15 you might feel the issue wasn't hotly debated. The discussion seems to proceed rather smoothly to an easy decision. But Galatians reveals how deeply entrenched were the ideas of the participants. The passions were intense and the settlement of the issue may have seemed uncertain. Paul, however, was not a peace-at-any-price man when the fundamentals of Christianity were in the balance. The Acts narrative refers to vehement "dissension and disputation" (15:2).

The Galatians passage indicates that Paul had a private conference with the leadership of the Jerusalem church. Possibly these men were James, Peter, and John (Galatians 2:9). Moffatt's translation of Galatians 2:2 states:

> (It was in consequence of a revelation that I went up at all.) I submitted the gospel I am in the habit of preaching to the Gentiles, submitting it privately to the authorities, to make sure that my course of action would be and had been sound.

The Argument for Tradition

The arguments for the position held by the Judaizers as stated by Emil Balliet are as follows:

(1) God had chosen Israel, and the physical sign of that covenant was circumcision. Had God's law been abrogated? Had He changed His mind? (2) Jesus himself was a Jew and had submitted to all the Law's demands. Should His followers do less? (3) All the promises of redemption, including the Messiah, had come through Israel. Could they turn away from Israel and the promises of God and still claim the redemption those promises offered? (4) Circumcision, in a sense, was like taking the cross to follow Jesus. It was part of the price that must be paid. Were they unwilling to pay the price? (*Acts* [Springfield, Mo: Gospel Publishing House, 1972]).

The New Testament Answer

The answers to these arguments would be as follows as we find them in Galatians and Romans.

1. Yes, God spoke to Israel through the prophets, but now He has spoken to us through His Son who is superior in position and authority to any of the servants or covenants in Israel's past.

2. Yes, Jesus submitted to all the demands of the Law. But He became the "end of the law for righteousness to every one that believeth" (Romans 10:4).

3. Yes, the covenants and promises of the Messiah came through Israel. They pointed to and were fulfilled in Him. When we are accepted in Him these are embraced and validated in our relationship with Him.

4. Circumcision, as such, was not the objection. The objection was to make it a means of salvation; that would corrupt the gospel of grace. We would then be saved by the work of Christ *plus* the works of the Law (Ephesians 2:8-10).

Two Questions

These first-century Christians dealt with two questions central to their faith. The first had to do with salvation. How are people really saved? The second question facing the conference came out of the first. If we by faith become children of God, we are brothers of Jesus Christ. Then how are we related to others who also by faith become children of God? Are we now in the same family? Are we brothers?

These questions and their answers evidence the revolutionary nature of the Christian faith. Christ breaks down the barriers of race, class, and national origins that divide us.

Think Big

Pearl Buck tells of the little 5-year-old who was preparing to paint on a huge sheet of blank paper. She paused for a moment. "What is it?" she was asked. "Don't you know what you want to paint?" "I do know," she replied, "but I want to make it big, and first I have to think big."

And that's what the council in Jerusalem had to do; they needed to think big. To really think big we need to think God's thoughts—to take time to hear from Him through His Word and prayer.

The Jerusalem conferees gave themselves to their task and came through "thinking big." At the conclusion they said, in reporting on their decision: "For it seemed good to the Holy Ghost, and to us" (15:28). Let's take a little look at the council agenda. A threefold testimony was presented.

Testimony From an Upper Room Man

After lengthy discussion and debate with free expression given to the traditionalists, Peter arose to speak. Peter was recognized as the apostle of the circumcision (Galatians 2:7, 8). And yet he graciously spoke not as an authoritarian but as a Christian brother. Peter reminded his audience that his visit to the house of the Gentile Cornelius was of

God (Acts 15:7; 10:19, 20). The Holy Spirit came upon the Gentile Christians just as He had come upon the Hebrew Christians. The unmistakable signs were the seal of God's acceptance of the Gentiles without the works of the Law. Obviously then from God's point of view uncircumcised Gentiles were as acceptable to Him as circumcised Jews. There was "no difference" between them spiritually (15:9). Why should the church compel believers to be circumcised when God accepted them in their uncircumcision? And then came his *coup de grace.* "Why . . . put a yoke upon the neck of the disciples, which neither our fathers nor we were able to bear?" (v. 10).

Testimony From the Field

Peter's speech silenced the entire council. Their silence gave Barnabas and Saul opportunity to confirm Peter's testimony. Theirs was a simple report repeating their testimony given in Antioch (14:27) and in Jerusalem (15:4). That which was a first experience in Cornelius' house had been repeated over and over wherever they went among the Gentiles. If God was setting His seal through signs and wonders on a "free-from-the-law" gospel, who were they to place legal restrictions on the recipients?

Testimony From Scripture

Silence continued and then it was James' turn (not the apostle, but the brother of Jesus), to speak. He apparently was the moderator and he wisely laid the entire matter before the council, drawing freely from Scripture. Appealing to the Old Testament, he declared that Amos 9:11, 12 predicted the inclusion of Gentiles in God's saving program. (A portion of the prophecy remains unfulfilled. God is presently taking out a people—this is the Church. Rebuilding the tabernacle refers to the restoration of Israel. Winning the "residue of men" refers to the Millennial Age.) James said the Jewish Christians must stop hindering the Gentiles and let God have His way in the message of Jesus.

Wisdom Prevails

The matter seemed settled. But James was not only orthodox, he was also wise. He recommended that Judas and Silas accompany Paul and Barnabas bearing letters to the Gentile Christians. He suggested that, while the Gentile Christians should not be under excessive bondage, they should be warned to abstain from conduct that might cause Hebrew Christians to stumble.

The council singled out four prohibitions that were particularly offensive (Acts 15:20, 29). There should be moral behavior that would "adorn the doctrine." The Gentile Christians were to enjoy their freedom but not parade or flaunt it before others. In his letter to the Romans (chapters 14 and 15), Paul deals very effectively with this matter.

The Best Moderator

The council closed in unity and goodwill. The participants recognized that the true Moderator had been the Holy Spirit (Acts 15:28). He had illuminated the Word, made stubborn wills pliable, and kept the Church united.

The Better Way

Some troubles can be settled on our knees, alone with God, but others require Christian counsel and friendly participation. You will do better after being on your knees with godly friends, than on your tiptoes in self-sufficiency. In godly counselors there is safety.

Differences or no differences, the Christians assembled in Jerusalem wanted the mind of the Lord, and when that was made clear it became the mind of the church. Any group of God's people can know God's will, but if factions insist on winning their point, the group is on the road to disaster. Carnal contentions grieve the Spirit, bring barrenness in service, and failure in testimony. The great concern should not be our differences; what we do with them is the thing that counts.

What Does God Say?

The mind of the Lord is important. What God's Word tells us regarding vital issues is of significant consequence. While the lines had been sharply divided at Jerusalem, there may have been some who couldn't care less. "Circumcision or uncircumcision—what's all the fuss about? There's good in everyone," they might say. "What's so important about drawing such fine lines? Why fight about it?" But the issue at Jerusalem was vital. Christian freedom was at stake.

Free or Fettered

Spiritual freedom was purchased at Calvary. The council at Jerusalem gave further definition. The Epistles to the Romans and Galatians, in particular, clinch the New Testament position. The Protestant Reformation gave the great boost to spiritual freedom in the Middle Ages. "Ye shall know the truth, and the truth shall make you free" (John 8:32).

The council at Jerusalem is a model for all times. The Church was freed from the prejudices of the bigot, the arrogance of the self-righteous, and the yoke of the ritualist. How much disgrace would be spared the cause of Christ if contending members would seek cleansing from arrogance and intolerance.

Pushing or Braking

Many people, possibly thinking they are being helpful, stop the forward progress of the church. They remind me of the storekeeper who stood in front of his place of business greeting passersby. Suddenly he noticed a car slowly rolling down the street without a driver at the wheel. Running to the car, he jumped in and stepped on the brake, stopping the car with a jolt.

As he got out, pleased with his feat, a man reached the door. "Well," said the storekeeper with a smile, "I stopped it."

"Yes, I know," said the irate owner, "I was pushing it."

Churches have people who by lack of understanding, headstrong resistance, or unbridled criticism, slam on the brakes. Thank God for leaders like Peter, Paul, Barnabas, and James who rise to the occasion. Differences are settled, God's will is revealed, and the church once again regains momentum.

The decision made at the council was not arrived at solely on the basis of debate; the apostolic decision came as a result of guidance by the Holy Spirit. The statement by James is impressive: "It seemed good to the Holy Ghost, and to us" (15:28).

Welcome News

The letters with the news of the decisions were welcomed with great rejoicing among Gentile believers (15:31). Their liberty in Christ was confirmed. The Church had weathered the attacks from without; now it had weathered the storm of internal division. The soul-searching ordeal was over; the crisis was past. The Magna Carta of Christian liberty had been hammered out for the Church Age.

Judas and Silas remained for several days in Antioch. Imagine the joy and blessing that accompanied their ministry. *The Living Bible* states: "Then Judas and Silas, both being gifted speakers, preached long sermons to the believers, strengthening their faith" (15:32).

8   The Assault on Europe

Read: Acts 15:36 to 16:40

Of significance in the life and ministry of the great missionary-apostle Paul is the fact that he associated himself with younger workers in the ministry.

Among these were people such as Luke, Gaius, Mark, Timothy, Silas, Tychicus, and Trophimus. They were of a variety of backgrounds racially, culturally, and temperamentally. In this chapter we are introduced to Silas, Timothy, and Lydia, and shortly we'll meet Priscilla and Aquila.

A Scrub, Maybe . . . but a Quitter, Never

Edward L. R. Elson tells the story of the remarkable monument on a midwestern university campus erected in honor of a student. This student had never won a prize or an election. His scholastic grades averaged a B. Every year he went out for football but never made the team or participated in an important game.

Serving in the Medical Corps in World War I, the former student was killed trying to rescue a wounded man under fire. The French conferred a *Croix de Guerre* on him. His university put up a monument with a most significant inscription on it: "He played four years on the scrubs, but he never quit."

Following the Jerusalem council, Paul proposed a second missionary trip to Barnabas. Barnabas agreed at once and was determined to take John Mark with them. Paul would not agree to this, apparently remembering how John Mark had deserted them on the first journey (13:13). "Their disagreement over this was so sharp that they separated" (15:39, *The Living Bible*).

Great Men May Disagree

The quarrel between these two good men seems regrettable, yet it did not hinder the gospel. On the contrary, it resulted in two missionary teams instead of one. Barnabas and John Mark sailed to Cyprus and Paul and his new team traveled overland through Syria and Cilicia.

Who was right in the dispute? Who was wrong? I don't know. Later Paul acknowledged Mark's worth (2 Timothy 4:11). And John Mark, the servant who *failed,* was chosen by the Lord to write the Gospel of the Servant who *never failed.*

Troubles Can Be Teachers

This episode of trouble has some excellent lessons for us. First, things never stay the same. Possibly many, including the two men themselves, expected that Paul and Barnabas would always team together. But change is inevitable.

Second, disappointment and disaster are not the end of everything. Both men probably wondered how things could ever be as good again.

Third, the will of God may be clouded, temporarily, at times.

A New Partner

When the partnership with Barnabas dissolved, Paul chose Silas to replace him. Silas was a "chief

[man] among the brethren" (15:22). A leader in his home church, Silas was also selected as qualified for the task because of his God-given wisdom and grace. He shared in bringing the results of the Jerusalem council to Antioch (15:22, 27).

The rift between Paul and Barnabas brought the opportunity of a lifetime to Silas. Paul chose him to be his partner on his second missionary trip. He appeared suddenly on the New Testament scene and disappeared as quickly after Paul's visit to Athens. The only other traces of him are the occasional references in the Epistles. Of special interest is the mention of him (Silvanus) as collaborator with Paul and Timothy in the writing of the two letters to the Thessalonians.

Silas and the other co-workers with Paul were not exactly "scrubs," but neither were they stars, such as Paul, on the team. They contributed greatly to God's work and did much to encourage and assist Paul, the "star" of the team.

A New Assistant

While Silas replaced Barnabas as Paul's partner, the vacancy left by John Mark had not yet been filled. Paul went to the scene of his greatest persecution, Derbe and Lystra, where he had been stoned and left for dead (14:19). There Paul found not only a replacement for John Mark in a young man named Timothy, but one who was also "as a son with the father" (Philippians 2:22).

Timothy had gained quick recognition for his Christian qualities both in his hometown and in neighboring Iconium. Although the child of a mixed marriage (his father being a Greek), Timothy's godly Jewish mother and grandmother had faithfully taught him the Scriptures. Fascinating details of his homelife are given in 2 Timothy 1:5; 3:14, 15.

Timothy was to become a mainstay in the church. When Paul penned his farewell Epistle to Timothy, written close to the time of his martyrdom, he committed the torch of truth to his beloved son in the faith, confident that Timothy would be its trusted advocate and guardian.

Producing Greatness

A mark of the greatness of Paul was his ability to develop greatness in others. To attain solitary prominence may be conspicuous; to bring others along is greatness. Timothy became more than a historical person; he is a proverb. As Jonah stands for a jinx and Judas for a traitor, you hear the expression, "He's my Timothy."

When God Says, "No"

Paul with his worthy companions, Silas and Timothy, traveled among the churches where he had ministered on his first trip. The decisions of the Jerusalem council were delivered and the churches were "established in the faith, and increased in number daily" (Acts 16:5). Evidently, Paul had desired to preach the gospel in Asia (the western section of Asia Minor). But God had other plans. The Holy Spirit restrained him. Then he turned his thoughts toward Bithynia, on the Black Sea. This seemed to be logical, but again the Spirit said, "No."

The walk to Troas (16:8) must have been one of new learning experiences. Human reasonings must yield to the directives of the Spirit. But that walk of obedience and faith brought a totally new course in the outreach of the young Apostolic Church.

Where We Come In

Acts 16 should hold very special interest to all of us in the Western world. Up until the events in this chapter, all attention had focused on the East. But now an event transpired that brought the gospel to our ancestors. Paul was intent on continued evangelistic efforts in Asia but he received a supernatural call at Troas that changed the course of missions and made all history different.

How different the ways of God from ours! Paul looked to Asia; God chose Europe. David Livingstone wanted to go to China; God sent him to Africa. Adoniram Judson selected India; God placed him in Burma. My wife and I looked toward the West for ministry. God sent us to Minnesota where I ended up becoming the district superintendent and later the president of North Central Bible College.

Negative . . . Positive

The Spirit had guided the preaching party negatively by *forbidding* in Galatia and Mysia (16:6, 7), but at Troas Paul received *positive* guidance. Between the Spirit's "no" and the vision at Troas, there had been a long period of silence for the preacher who continually overflowed with his message. One can only speculate as to what lessons were learned during this long, tedious journey. Let's remember that the Lord keeps testing our faith and obedience. As we faithfully follow His leadings, even though they are but checks, He will bring us to the place of fulfillment in His will.

Hearing From Heaven

At Troas, God spoke to Paul in a vision. Before him came a man calling, "Come over into Macedonia, and help us" (16:9). Now Paul understood the checks of the Spirit. He shared the conviction that he should minister in Europe with his associates and found them in agreement. The decision was to proceed "immediately" and they sailed from Troas, "assuredly gathering that the Lord had called us for to preach the gospel unto them" (16:10).

The pronoun *we* emerges at Troas indicating that Luke, the writer of Acts, had joined the party. Luke, a physician (Colossians 4:14), was apparently the only Gentile among the New Testament writers.

The travels of the missionaries through Europe read like a romance. We follow them to Philippi, Thessalonica, Berea, Athens, and Corinth; and there were visits to many smaller places in between. Over and over Paul, in his mission of conquest, offered one message—Christ crucified, resurrected, and ascended to the right hand of the Father, from where He bestows His gifts.

European Firsts

Several European *firsts* appear in Acts 16. *First,* the first recorded impact for Christ in Europe. We should thank God every day that Paul obeyed the Macedonian call. And we ought to recognize our great debt and pray for a vision of souls in other lands who still cry, "Come over . . . and help us."

Second, the first converts in Europe—Lydia and her household (16:14, 15)—show us the place that godly, consecrated women have in the work of God.

Third, the first opposition in Europe (16:16-24) tells us that Paul's troubles with the Gentiles began when he touched their pocketbooks (v. 19).

Fourth, the first miracles (16:18, 25, 26) evidenced the mighty power of the Holy Spirit who works with those who believe in God and walk by faith.

Fifth, the establishment of the first church in Europe. The church of Philippi, to which Paul, as a prisoner in Rome, wrote his blessed "joybook," the Epistle to the Philippians, must have had as "charter" members Lydia and her family, the demon-delivered girl, and the jailer and his family.

A Church Without Walls

The first extensive ministry in Europe was in Philippi, a leading Macedonian city that had originally been settled by Roman veterans and their families. Since the Jews, being few in number, had no religious meeting place like the synagogue, a place of prayer was used by a riverside. Here devout women gathered.

The urging of the Spirit to go to Europe came in a vision of a "man from Macedonia" calling. Strange are God's ways! The "man" turned out to be a group of women in a ladies' prayer meeting.

Among the women who gathered was a wealthy businesswoman from Thyatira. Her city was famous for its dyeworks, and especially for producing the purple cloth so much in demand in fashion circles at that time. She was a worshiper of God, apparently as a Jewish proselyte. Her appreciation for spiritual matters is indicated by her association with this little group at the riverbank rather than mingling with the crowds thronging the heathen temple.

As Paul preached, the Lord opened her heart (16:14). God brought more color and beauty into her life than all the beautiful tints of the expensive dyes she sold. Those who worship God put themselves in a place for God to deal with them.

Open Heart . . . Home . . . Purse

Lydia is not mentioned again in the Bible, but the brief reference in verses 14 and 15 leaves us some rich gems. She was a wealthy woman with an *open heart*, an *open home*, and an *open purse*. When God opened her heart, she evidenced her conversion and love for God by opening her home and her pocketbook and constraining the four preachers to be her guests during their ministry in Philippi (16:15). Her offer of hospitality was made with great tact. Their stay in her home would not be a burden to her, but a privilege to demonstrate the sincerity of her faith; she would be the beneficiary.

Very possibly the generosity of Lydia created a spirit of liberality that prevailed in the church. While in prison many years later, Paul wrote: "You Philippians became my partners in giving and receiving. No other church did this" (Philippians 4:15, *The Living Bible*).

Winning the Beachhead

The beachhead for the gospel was won at the riverside in Philippi. The counterattack followed quickly. The beachhead had been taken easily, but the enemy soon had his forces in full action. The struggle between truth and error centered on a girl with an evil spirit. Vested interests opposed the missionaries.

The demon-possessed young lady was the puppet of what was probably a syndicate of money-mad men who exploited her for their own profit. On the surface it may have seemed she did no damage, for her testimony regarding the missionaries was true (16:17). But God doesn't invite testimony from those whose association with that testimony would discredit its influence. Led by the Spirit, Paul exposed and cast out the evil spirit.

The reaction was violent. Whenever the gospel encroaches on the pocketbook of God's enemies they begin to fight. Paul and Silas were mercilessly beaten and thrown into prison. They received this cruel treatment for doing right!

Preearthquake

Although imprisoned on trumped-up, illegal

charges, Paul and Silas were able to bear their testimony for Christ with grace. They sang hymns in their prison cell, "and the prisoners heard them" (16:25).

Earthquake

The prison couldn't keep men who "prayed, and sang praises unto God." The place shook with a great earthquake and all the doors opened. The jailer, fearing the prisoners had escaped, was about to commit suicide rather than face Roman execution. But upon Paul's assurance that they were all there, the Roman jailer posed life's greatest question: "Sirs, what must I do to be saved?" (16:30).

Postearthquake

The jailer gladly grasped Paul's response. He believed on the Lord Jesus Christ. Then he washed their stripes, and with his household was baptized. This is one of three cases of household salvation and baptism related in Acts; the others were Cornelius' and Lydia's households. How wonderful when the influence of the home reaches every member!

Have you noticed the contrasts in conversions? Lydia's conversion was quite different from that of the jailer. Hers was quiet; his was noisy. The simple preaching of the Word opened her heart; the jailer went through a great earthquake and was on the verge of suicide. But he too responded to the Word, and the same grace and power regenerated and transformed them both.

Paul used his Roman citizenship to advantage. He refused to leave the prison on his own. He demanded the magistrates themselves come and lead him and Silas out; which they did for fear of what they had done to Roman citizens (16:35-39).

Heaven's artillery had defeated the enemy. The preachers were out of jail; the jailer and his family were now believers; the enemy was humiliated and crestfallen; and the beachhead in Europe was further strengthened.

9   Breaking New Ground

Read: Acts 17

"I went to a Bible study group with my wife. It was just a Bible study, but it angered me. I thought, 'These people talk like they have God in their hip pocket.' But I went eight Wednesdays in a row. The last Wednesday evening, while everyone was praying, I got down on my knees and gave my life to the Lord and I have never been the same since. It was an emotional experience, but it hasn't passed. That was nine years ago."

That's the testimony of Lee Buck, a senior vice-president of the New York Life Insurance Company, as quoted in *Time* magazine (December 26, 1977). Where was the testimony given? In an old-fashioned evangelical church? at a revival meeting? No, it was given in a "thoroughly Episcopal church in Darien, Connecticut."

Whether it's in the crumbling decay of the ghetto or the elegance of Fifth Avenue, the gospel works. Wherever Christ is preached in the power of the Spirit, changes take place. Everywhere Paul went with the good news, he "turned the world upside down" (17:6).

Paul and his party arrived in Europe unknown and unheralded. But that anonymity didn't last long. As was often the case, he and his party ended up in jail.

78

The early Christians, especially the apostles, found this to be almost routine. But they brought redeeming change to the cities they visited.

Going to Church or Being the Church

I wouldn't invite a "jailbird" experience, but I often wonder if we prefer respectability to aggressive evangelism. Isn't much of our commitment synthetic? We "go to church" instead of "being the church."

After his exciting adventures in Philippi, Paul went on to Thessalonica, passing through Amphipolis and Apollonia on the way. Amphipolis, a busy and strategic center and the capital of the first district of Macedonia, was 33 miles from Philippi. Apollonia, another 30 miles further, was a lovely wooded city. Paul was not directed to plant churches in either one, but to walk 37 miles more to Thessalonica, a busy harbor and naval base with a population of 200,000.

Joining God's Squad

Following his normal pattern, Paul went to the local synagogue where he taught for three Sabbaths. He was forced to leave the synagogue to continue in private homes for approximately 6 months. All the while he supported himself by making tents (1 Thessalonians 2:9). Paul presented the crucified, resurrected Christ, laying the prophecies concerning the Messiah alongside the life of Jesus, presenting and proving the messiahship of Jesus.

The Scriptures indicate that a "great multitude" of godly Greeks, including many important women, and a few Jews believed in the living Christ (Acts 17:4).

Up Against a Goon Squad

The devil, however, was not asleep. By and large, the Jews rejected the gospel of the Messiah. They incited a riot, drawing the common rabble into the uproar. Rowdies loafing in the marketplace led in the disorder. When the rioters couldn't find Paul and Silas, they vented their wrath on Jason, in whose house the missionary team lodged. The mob dragged Jason to the city authorities and brought charges against Paul and Silas (17:5-9).

Upside Down

"These that have turned the world upside down are come hither also" (v. 6). What a compliment! And that's what God's servants are to do: We are to upset the world that it might be set right again. Have you ever turned your neighbors upside down for Christ—with love and tact, of course—by your testimony?

The accusers of Jesus tried to cover their envy by accusing Him of stirring up the people. God's enemies in every age have followed the tactic of sending up a smoke screen of false charges by which to attack His servants. Some claim the gospel is divisive; others hide behind the pretense of intellectual objection to certain doctrines. The worldly bow to the authority of the god of this world. They resent anything that upsets their complacency.

Gravitation and Magnetism

Gravitation and magnetism are two forces that work in the same fields without conflict, so the claims of Christ as King of kings are readily accepted by Christians who are loyal subjects of earthly nations. Sheer envy and self-seeking motives prompted the unbelieving Jews to raise false charges and precipitate a riot.

If our religion never upsets anyone we might well ask ourselves if we are really Christians. Preaching from Acts 17:6, a country preacher made the following outline for his sermon: (1) The world was at first right side up. (2) Sin came and turned it upside down. (3) The world has got to be set right again. (4) We're the chaps to do it.

Making a Fizzle

Too many of us are like the blacksmith Lincoln used to tell about. He heated a piece of iron in the forge and started to hammer it into a horseshoe. Before he finished he changed his mind and started to make something else. After a little more hammering he changed his mind again and started something else. A little more of this and he had hammered the iron so it was not much good for anything. At last in disgust he thrust it hissing into a tub of water and exclaimed, "Well, at least I can make a fizzle out of it."

Paul made no fizzle. He was never dismayed when enemies appeared. He was always aware his message might cause hostility, but he continued on expecting to achieve God's purpose in the good soil of receptive hearts. If we will take our directions daily from God, we may turn some things upside down too.

Glory in the Grind

Crisis and continuance are earmarks of a Spirit-filled Christian. Lofty experiences, high days, ecstatic happenings—thank God for them, but to run on such a track can lead to excesses and a nerve-straining high pitch. On the other hand, a stolid walk can leave you in a rut. Someone said, "Tasks in hours of *insight* willed, can be in hours of *gloom* fulfilled." That's what Luke wrote of Paul's Macedonian call:

"After he had seen the vision, immediately we endeavored to go" (16:10). And they kept going with the vision in focus. Vance Havner states, "As important as the Grandeur of Getting Started is the Grace of Going On." That's the vision and the venture; it's the glory that shows up in the grind.

Run Out of Town

In view of the existing temper in Thessalonica, the only way to preserve the peace was to send Paul and his party out of the city. The little company that had successfully hidden them, spirited them out of the city by night. Still following the Roman road, Paul and Silas trudged on through the night and eventually reached Berea, an inland town 45 to 50 miles southwest of Thessalonica.

Never Retreat

Wouldn't you think that after the harrowing experiences in Philippi and Thessalonica it was time for a little rest? But not for Paul! He never sounded retreat. Fear was never evidenced and cowardice was unknown to him. The great soldier shunned furloughs and never even took a brief "R and R."

Where do we find Paul in Berea? In the synagogue, of course. And what was he doing? Preaching and teaching the Word of God. What else would you expect? And here Paul found very encouraging results. Many believed, including prominent women (17:10-12).

Marks of Nobility

The Bereans "were more noble" than the Thessalonians. Their nobility had no reference to natural birth, but rather to their receptivity to the gospel. Two things marked the Bereans. *First*, "They received the Word with all readiness of mind" (17:11).

The Word was welcomed with enthusiasm. They were ready to listen; their minds were open. When people have no prejudice, the soil is ready to receive the good seed of the Word. What a joy it must have been to preach to the Bereans!

Second, the Bereans "searched the Scriptures daily, whether those things were so" (17:11). They were systematic in their study of the Word. The Bible-reading Bereans checked to make certain Paul's teaching found credence in God's authority and to be sure their own faith rested on a solid foundation. If only people today would use the Bible as habitually as the Bereans and saturate their minds with divine truth.

Long Distance

There is a superficial reading of the Bible that reminds us of the new maid who, strange as it may seem, had never been around a telephone. "Well, Rhoda," asked her employer, "did anyone call while I was out?" "Yes," said Rhoda with a laugh, "there was some crackpot who called and said, 'Long distance from Los Angeles,' but I just told her I knew that and hung up." You can imagine her feelings when she learned the meaning of the call. How often our knowledge of the Word is shallow and our responses flippant.

The Bereans have left an enduring stamp on the Church. Untold thousands have been members of Berean classes in Sunday schools and other church study groups. What a tribute to Christians in an isolated inland town of long ago!

What a Farewell Party

Paul's farewell parties were something else. As a rule, when a pastor leaves a congregation, the church plans a lovely farewell gathering. The pastor and his family take their leave with the love of the people and an appropriate gift. Paul always left with the loving concern of his parishioners. But his leave-taking had to be sudden and secretive: "The brethren immediately sent away Paul and Silas by night" from Thessalonica (17:10). Mass opposition was kindled in Berea by Thessalonian Jews who had followed the missionaries the nearly 50 miles. Paul's escape had fanned their fury into a flame and they were determined to stop his work. Again, "The brethren sent away Paul to go as it were to the sea" (17:14). Not a very flattering farewell party. Fortunately for the Berean church, Silas and Timothy were able to remain with them.

When He Saw

Paul was brought by his Berean friends to Athens. Immediately Paul sent word for Silas and Timothy to join him. We find him alone, waiting for them. To plant a church in Athens was not his plan. But Paul couldn't just wait "when he saw the city" (17:16). What did he see?

Athens was one of the three great centers of that world. Jerusalem was the religious center, Rome the political center, and Athens the cultural and intellectual center. New centers had risen to displace Athens (such as Antioch, Tarsus, Ephesus, and especially Alexandria), but Athens was still considered the hub of philosophic learning.

In Athens, human ability had attained its highest. The city abounded with philosophers and schools of learning. To this day the names of Socrates, Plato, Aristotle, Pericles, and Phidias—great Athenian philosophers, writers, and artists—are common to college students everywhere. At one time, according to the historian Pliny, 3,000 public statues graced the city with thousands more in private homes and gardens. Today's visitor to Athens sees "the glory that was Greece." The ancient ruins tell the story of a city of magnificent grandeur and beauty.

But Paul was overcome with an emotion other than admiration. In this great city he saw a wilderness of pagan cults and idol shrines. The most degrading forms of licentious idolatry existed side by side with intellectual snobbery.

Gospel at *Agora*

The apostle could not be idle while awaiting Silas and Timothy. He was never content to set up his defenses and wait for the devil to attack; he chose to assume the offensive and challenge the entrenchments of pagan culture. He not only exercised his witness in the synagogue, but also in the marketplace *(agora)* where public discussions were a daily routine. An audience was assured: "For all the Athenians, and strangers which were there, spent their time in nothing else, but either to tell or to hear some new thing" (17:21).

The philosophers of Athens were motivated by boundless, frivolous curiosity with no sense of personal need. Let's look at his audience: "Philosophers" who exalted human wisdom and reasoning; "Epicureans" who lived to please the senses and made a god of pleasure; and "Stoics" who worshiped at the shrine of self, making a god out of virtue and self-discipline.

Seed-picker

These men looked on Paul as an amateur philosopher and in scorn dubbed him a "babbler" (literally, a "seed-picker" or one who has learned a crude smattering of knowledge picked up here and there). They seized him, bringing him to Mars' Hill and demanded him to explain these novel ideas of "Jesus" and the "resurrection."

A Masterpiece

Paul stood in the very center of the world's culture, in an atmosphere heavy with proud sophistication and base idolatry, and preached (17:22-31). His sermon was a masterpiece. At home with the most brilliant philosophers, Paul met the challenge of Athenian wisdom and idolatry. The reasoning of the Athenian philosophers brought them to nothing. They were left face-to-face with the unknown and the unknowable. Where the philosophers left off, Paul began—". . . THE UNKNOWN GOD. Whom therefore ye ignorantly worship, him declare I unto you" (v. 23).

The apostle dealt two deathblows to idolatry: the first, the argument from the nature of God; the second, the argument from the nature of man. Idolatry is incompatible with the nature of God (17:24-27). Idolatry is incompatible with the nature of man (17:28, 29). From there Paul proved idolatry is incompatible with the gospel (17:30, 31).

In essence, Paul declared we are the offspring of deity—which even the Athenian poets acknowledged. And if we are God's creation, God must be a Spirit. If so, why compare Him to "gold or silver" or worship images of marble engraved by men?

Further, man's needs go far beyond idol worship. He is a sinner. God has been patient, but now He commands "all men every where to repent" (v. 30). The Judge has been appointed. His appointment has been ratified by His resurrection from the dead.

The Reaction

The reaction to the message was threefold: (1) Some mocked as they heard of the resurrection; (2)

Others procrastinated, saying, "We will hear thee again of this matter"; and (3) Some believed. One was a judge of the court; another was a woman of some importance.

And then there were "others." While there were converts, neither the canonical nor the noncanonical writings leave a record of an established church. It does seem that Paul determined the philosophical approach, now that he was in the Greek world, was not the answer. Perhaps, if that be so, we understand his complete abandonment to the one great theme, "Jesus Christ, and him crucified," that gripped his soul as he went on to Corinth (1 Corinthians 2:2).

10 Taking Great Cities

Read: Acts 18 and 19

In Philippi Paul had been unmercifully whipped by order of the judges, without any form of trial, and heartlessly thrown into prison. At Thessalonica an angry mob, thirsting for his blood, came to the home where he was a guest, and he was forced to run for his life at night, after a beautiful experience of seeing multitudes come to Christ. His Thessalonian enemies tracked him to Berea and again he had to escape for his life. At Athens his preaching was met with ridicule by some and indifference by others.

Harrassed . . . Slandered . . . Ridiculed

"After these things Paul departed from Athens, and came to Corinth" (18:1). Harrassed by his enemies, misrepresented to government authorities, slandered by those of his own race, ridiculed by the academic community—what obstacles! What dauntless courage, fervent zeal, and dogged determination! Driven here and there by overwhelming difficulties, the apostle persevered, leaving a trail of converts and churches.

Facing a Cesspool

No vision summoned Paul to Corinth. But his coming to this great city, the largest and most important in Greece, was to be marked by weighty consequences both for himself and the cause of the gospel.

Located about 50 miles west of Athens and boasting a population of some 400,000, Corinth was a new city built by Julius Caesar on the same site as the old Corinth which had been lying in ruins for a century. While Athens was the cultural center, Corinth was the commercial center. Its reputation for licentiousness and immorality was worldwide. The term *Corinthian* had become a synonym for shameless disregard of decency and depraved abandon of moral restraint.

Facing a Crisis

Paul's first days in Corinth were a crisis period for him. He had been laughed out of Athens and left there never to return. Violent persecution was a part of his life and ministry wherever he went. Always he was able to rise above it and joyfully keep going. But Athens had given him something worse than violent opposition—his message had roused neither interest nor opposition. The proud, arrogant Athenians simply didn't care what this "seed-picker" had to say. Athens must have been a disappointment to Paul.

When Paul came to Corinth he was alone, without friends or acquaintances. Possibly he dreaded a repeat of his reception at Athens. The people of these wicked prosperous cities appeared to feel no wants. Paul arrived in Corinth "in weakness, and in fear, and in much trembling" (1 Corinthians 2:3).

Why Corinth?

Paul had nerve to go there. But he had more; he had God! What a strategic place. A stream of travelers, merchants, scholars, and sailors passed through this great commercial city. The message preached here would be carried to the ends of the earth. God shook the city through His servant Paul and made it a new center for the spreading of the gospel.

Athens was the symbol of intellect and art. Corinth was the symbol of immorality in its worst forms. In Athens Paul left only a handful of converts. In Corinth "much people" became Christians. How often this picture is repeated. Again and again those steeped in sin recognize their need of a Saviour much more readily than the self-sufficient who pride themselves on their intellectual attainments.

Teaming Up

In the year A.D. 52, the year Paul arrived in Corinth, Emperor Claudius issued a cruel decree ordering all Jews to leave Rome. While this uprooting caused misery for a lot of innocent people, it was providential for at least three persons—Paul, Aquila, and his wife Priscilla. The latter two had arrived just before Paul. They were tentmakers as was Paul. The apostle sought employment at his old trade to support himself. Soon he and the two exiles from Rome found themselves working together. Priscilla and Aquila were turned to the Lord and became great friends of Paul and supporters of his ministry (Acts 18:1-4).

The Jerusalem church had the covetous, scheming couple, Ananias and Sapphira, on whom judgment fell under the ministry of Peter. But now another husband-and-wife team came on the scene. What a great team they became (Acts 18:18, 19, 24-26; Romans 16:3-5; 1 Corinthians 16:19; 2 Timothy 4:19). They were with him in Ephesus. Later, on hearing the eloquent Apollos, they sensed his lack. With tact they "expounded unto him the way of God more perfectly"—not criticism but exposition (Acts 18:26). It was the same "way of God," but "more perfectly" explained. Paul paid them a glowing tribute: "I give thanks, . . . also all the churches" for Priscilla and Aquila (Romans 16:3-5).

Refreshing News

When Silas and Timothy arrived from Macedonia, they found Paul busily preaching and teaching. His friends brought good news. The churches were thriving and the Philippian church sent him an offering. Paul took new strength and courage and plunged full time into ministry. With great earnestness he "testified to the Jews that Jesus was Christ" (18:5).

Opposition by the Jews became abusive. They were willful, deliberate, and united in their refusal to receive Paul's message concerning Christ. In their unbelief they went so far as to hurl not only insults but also blasphemies (v. 6).

A Turning Point

Rebuffed by the Jewish people, Paul shook off the dust from his robe in the typical gesture of the times (Matthew 10:14). This was a significant moment in the history of the Church. Paul declared that from then on he would preach to the Gentiles (18:6). He withdrew from the synagogue and began holding services in the house of a man named Titus Justus, a convert who lived next door to the synagogue. Crispus, the leader of the synagogue, and all his household believed, as did many others (18:8).

It Came at Night

The Lord knew all about Paul—his struggles and trials, his weariness in mind and body, and all that lay before him by way of hardship and suffering. In the night, at the darkest hour, Paul heard God's voice. In essence, God said, "Go on preaching, Paul. I am with you. You and I are a majority in Corinth and no harm will come to you. I have a lot of people in this city." The strain had been severe and even Paul had become discouraged, but God was with him (18:9, 10).

So Paul stayed in Corinth for 18 months. He settled down to preaching and teaching the Word with a restfulness of mind after the assuring and comforting revelation from the Lord. During this time Paul wrote 1 and 2 Thessalonians.

Thrown Out of Court

One of the difficulties faced by the Christian witness is unbelief. Paul found this in Corinth and particularly when he was brought before Gallio, the governor of Achaia. Gallio was the brother of Seneca, the famous philosopher who was Nero's teacher. Hardly had Gallio arrived to take over his appointment than the Jews stormed into his court, dragging in Paul, and accusing the apostle of teaching doctrine contrary to the law. Argument was hot and the question of justice was prominent (18:14). As they split hairs over words, Gallio turned from Roman to Hebrew law. Gallio "threw the case out of court." At this time Rome had no concern regarding Christians. This decision was equivalent to a charter for the Christians to preach the gospel throughout the empire.

Time to Move

Eighteen months had passed. There had been none of the bloody opposition that Paul had met in other cities. The time to move on had come. Paul could leave with the satisfaction that the church at Corinth was one of the strongest he had established. His two letters to the Corinthians give us rich insights into the church and list many of Paul's converts.

The second missionary journey drew to a close as Paul left Europe and stopped briefly in Ephesus with a promise to return later. He hurried to Jerusalem (18:22) and then returned to his home base at Antioch—his second missionary tour was completed.

A New Partner

The story of Paul and his ministry is interrupted to introduce a new partner, Apollos. Born in Alexandria, Apollos had come to Ephesus before Paul began his 3 years of ministry there. An ardent student and a keen thinker, Apollos was a noted orator and "mighty in the Scriptures" (18:24).

Apollos was led into the deeper fellowship of the Spirit through the humble lives and God-blessed instruction of Priscilla and Aquila. Apollos was humble and ready to sit at the feet of these godly tentmakers. Through their competent teaching Apollos became "more perfectly" instructed in the "way of God" and was greatly used of God.

8,100 Miles

Paul was ready to begin his third missionary tour. It is estimated the first journey was 1,400 miles long, the second 3,200, and the third 3,500, totaling 8,100 miles traveled by Paul. The time taken for the three tours was about 10 years. The Biblical record of these journeys is given in 8½ chapters in Acts (13:1 to 21:17). (References are also made to these in Romans 15:19 and 2 Corinthians 11:24-27.) Some scholars believe Paul was released at the end of his 2-year imprisonment in Rome (Acts 28:30) and he traveled as far east as Colossae and as far west as Spain.

On the Road Again

The ending of the second tour and the beginning of the third are tied together in Acts 18:22, 23. Paul once again toured Galatia and Phrygia, visiting the churches he had pioneered on his first trip. These were the same churches he had visited at the outset of his second tour. On the second trip he had wanted to take the gospel to the province of Asia where Ephesus was located, but the Holy Spirit had directed otherwise. Now, traveling through Turkey, he arrived at Ephesus (19:1).

A Look at Ephesus

If Corinth was a byword for debauchery, it had a close rival in Ephesus. Among Eastern cities, Ephesus was second in size to Alexandria. Its Temple of Artemis (Diana) was one of the seven wonders of the ancient world. According to ancient writers who had seen the Hanging Gardens of Babylon, the Colossus of Rhodes, and the pyramids of Egypt, none compared to the Temple of Artemis. It has been called the most impressive structure ever made by man. Measuring 425 feet long by 220 feet wide, it had 127 columns, each 60 feet high, and each a gift of a king.

Ephesus spawned the first bank and brimmed with Roman power and splendor. On the western slope of the city the Greeks had built one of their largest amphitheaters, with a seating capacity for some 50,000 people. It was truly a great city and one Paul wanted to reach with the gospel.

The church founded in Ephesus through the labors of Paul was only one of a circuit that were planted. Seven of these were the recipients of the letters from Patmos as given to John and recorded in Revelation. Both John and Luke spent their later years in Ephesus.

A Pointed Question

On his arrival in Ephesus, Paul met 12 men who had been converted as a result of Apollos' preaching.

Discerning in them a lack of spiritual power, Paul asked a straightforward question: "Have ye received the Holy Ghost since ye believed?" (19:2). Upon finding they had never heard of the Holy Spirit and had been baptized "unto John's baptism," he baptized them. Then as Paul laid hands on them, "the Holy Spirit came on them, and they spoke in tongues and prophesied" (19:6, *NIV*).

Several things are evident: (1) Paul's question indicates the baptism in the Holy Spirit is an experience distinct from conversion. The teaching of other Scripture bears this out; (2) It is evident that believers were taught to receive the fullness of the Spirit immediately upon conversion; and (3) The baptism in the Spirit was the normal experience for believers.

The outpouring of the Spirit in Ephesus is the last of five instances recorded in the Book of Acts. Three are described in detail (2:4; 10:44-47; 19:6), one in part (8:14-18), and the other only inferred (9:17; 1 Corinthians 14:18). From this record we get our understanding of what took place when believers were baptized in the Holy Spirit in the Apostolic Church. In every case where the details are given, speaking in tongues is always mentioned.

Moving to a Schoolhouse

For 3 months Paul preached on the Sabbath in the synagogue. Many believed but others were hardened. Paul then moved to a schoolhouse—the school of Tyrannus (Acts 19:9). The business hours in the cities of the East ended by the middle of the day. Probably Paul taught in this lecture hall in the afternoons when officials, lawyers, shopkeepers, and craftsmen could attend.

Special Miracles

During this time the Lord came to the aid of His

servant in another way: "God wrought special miracles by the hands of Paul: so that from his body were brought unto the sick handkerchiefs or aprons [literally sweat-rags and work aprons], and the diseases departed from them, and the evil spirits went out of them" (19:11, 12).

Exorcists Beware

The wizards and sorcerers of Ephesus took note of the miracles of Paul. Knowing that he did all things in the name of Jesus, they attempted to use that same Name in their spells. Their attempt backfired. Instead of advancing their reputation, they were made a laughingstock, besides sustaining physical hurt (19:13-16).

The Big Fire

The story of what happened spread quickly. Fear came on the city and the name of the Lord Jesus was magnified. Many believed and exponents of sorcery brought their books, worth about $10,000, and burned them at a public bonfire (19:17-20).

A Big Blowup

A big blowup developed in Ephesus. The spread of the gospel was making inroads into industries supported by the heathen practices in Diana's temple. The craftsmen were feeling the pinch. Demetrius, a leader of the silversmiths, attempted to piously uphold the honor of Diana, all the while making his pitch because of his diminishing profits (19:24-27).

The city was thrown into confusion. But God saved His faithful servants by causing the town clerk to become an unwitting tool in God's hand. He made a speech that soon dispersed the crowd (19:35-41).

Prophets or Profits?

Have you considered how much we are stimulated by prophets and profits? These were the drives at work in Ephesus when Paul came into confrontation with the syndicate headed by Demetrius. Demetrius was primarily concerned with financial profits; Paul's concern was spiritual gains. How many people play on religious and patriotic sentiments for their own gain!

11 Journey Into Danger

Read: Acts 20:1 to 23:10

Paul lived in the eye of a tornado, from that day on the Damascus road until he was beheaded in Rome. But he was serene, calm, and quietly confident in the center of the storm. He never wavered, never doubted, and never gave way to fear or despair. His composure was as amazing as his courage.

Francis of Assisi, hoeing in his garden, was asked what he would do if he were to suddenly discover he was to die at sunset that day. His reply? "I would finish hoeing my garden." What a great way to live! That's the way Paul lived.

Do what you have to do. Finish your course. The Master awaits you at the end.

Paying the Rent

Service is the rent we pay, someone has said, for the space we occupy in life. Follow Paul's life and ministry and you'd think he paid rent for that space for years to come.

Wherever Paul preached the gospel he stirred up a commotion. Luke uses words like "uproar," "rioting," and "confusion" to describe what happened.

Yet Paul wasn't a rabble-rouser. He didn't seek sensation. He simply preached God's truth; but people preferred to keep God's truth out of their lives. He preached Christ as Saviour of all, but some wanted to confine salvation to a select few. Herod slew male children because of Jesus. John the Baptist was beheaded for pointing to the Way. Peter was thrown in jail. Paul bore in his "body the marks of the Lord Jesus" (Galatians 6:17). He cites the price he paid in 2 Corinthians 11:21-28.

If I had to choose between preaching that lulls me to sleep and the dynamite that explodes something great in my soul—I'd choose the dynamite!

Building Roads

There is a story to the effect that a certain society once wrote to David Livingstone: "Have you found a good road to where you are? If so, we want to send other men to join you."

Livingstone replied, "If you have men who will come only if they know there is a good road, I don't want them. I want men strong and courageous, who will come if there is no road at all."

Paul was a road builder; he opened roads to God for 20 centuries of wandering, lost travelers. The impassable stretches and other perils of the road never deterred him. Again and again he built roads through hostile, enemy territory where there had been no road before. The unknown in the distance, instead of frightening him, drew him on. Paul refused to build on the foundation of others. He was always leaving churches behind for others to build upon. As death approached he was still dreaming of conquering new territories in the most remote corners of his world (Romans 15:24).

Paul launched his third missionary tour as he had his first two, from his home base, Antioch in Syria. The ending, however, was not as he had expected. While visiting Jerusalem before returning to Antioch, he was arrested.

More Than a Traveler

But now to continue reviewing his third journey. Paul was not only a missionary-evangelist who preached the good news; he was also an organizer and leader of people. Converts were always brought together and organized into a church. Again and again the churches he founded were visited. Trusted fellow workers were sent to instruct and encourage them. Letters were sent to them. On this third tour the first Epistle to the Corinthians was written from Ephesus, the second Epistle was penned in Macedonia (probably Philippi), and Galatians and Romans were authored at Corinth.

Eluding Murderers

Following ministry in Macedonia, Paul spent 3 months in Greece, possibly headquartering in Corinth. What reunions there must have been in all these churches! As always, Paul's bitter enemies, who considered him a traitor and deserter, schemed to harm him (Acts 20:3). Upon hearing that Corinthian Jews planned to murder Paul on his embarkation, he eluded the conspirators by going by land to Philippi.

From Philippi, Paul and Luke took a ship for Troas. Apparently they encountered difficulty. The trip normally took 48 hours, but Luke indicates it took 5 days. On arriving in Troas, Paul and Luke were reunited with their other traveling companions (20:4, 5).

These other men were going with Paul to carry the offering that had been collected from among the Gentile Christians to relieve the poverty-stricken among the believers in the Jerusalem church. At the council in Jerusalem, the elders had exhorted Paul not to forget the poor. For 2 years or more the Gentile churches in Galatia (1 Corinthians 16:1), Asia (Acts

20:4), Macedonia (Acts 20:4; 2 Corinthians 9:2), and Greece (2 Corinthians 9:2) had worked on this project. Paul wisely chose not to touch the offerings, but to delegate the responsibility to seven men chosen from among the churches.

Preaching Until Midnight

Seven days were spent at Troas. On Sunday the church gathered for a Communion service. Paul and his companions took advantage of the opportunity to meet with the believers that evening. The occasions afforded them to hear the beloved Paul were few. As Paul preached, the hours passed. Apparently hunger for the Word was great, for no complaints are recorded. Paul was still preaching at midnight when a young man by the name of Eutychus fell asleep. Seated on a windowsill, he fell three stories to his death. But Paul was there and the power of God was present. Eutychus was brought back to life. They all returned to the room and remained in worship until daybreak (Acts 20:7-12).

An Emotional Good-bye

Paul was hurrying to return to Jerusalem in time for Pentecost. But he didn't want to leave Asia Minor without saying good-bye to his beloved Ephesians. His 3 years of ministry there gave him endearing memories. Yet to go to the city proper would have taken too much time, so he sent a message to the church, and the elders traveled the 28 miles to Miletus.

The reunion with these dear friends was touching. Paul knew he would never see them again (20:38). He was aware the church would be threatened from without and within by false teachers and apostates. Knowing that great responsibilities would rest on these men he made a personal, passionate plea that they shepherd the flock faithfully and remain alert against insidious attacks (20:17-38).

A Farewell Message

The farewell message can be capsuled into three major divisions:

1. *Confidence for the present* (20:17-21). He reviewed his past ministry with them, calling attention to the spirit of his ministry despite bitter opposition and to the diligence of his ministry in teaching all the essential doctrines. He touched on his toil (20:18, 20, 21, 31), tears (20:19, 31), and temptations (20:19).

2. *Preparations for the future* (20:22-27). His future was secure despite predicted trials (20:22-24). His record was clean (20:25, 26) and his conscience was clear (20:27).

3. *Remembering the past* (20:28-38). His parting charge (20:28-32) is very fitting for any pastor. The specific charge in verse 28 covers the entire scope of pastoral ministry: "Take heed . . . unto [yourself]"—the minister's *personal, private* life. "Take heed . . . to all the flock"—the minister's *public* life, ministering to all. "Take heed . . . to feed the church of God"—the minister's *pulpit* life. Why be careful to feed the Church? Because it is purchased at such great cost—"with his own blood."

The apostle urged the elders to *watch*. He shared a last reminder (20:33-35) and a final prayer (20:36-38). Tears flowed freely and the great apostle knelt with his beloved friends and commended them to God. They embraced him and sadly followed him down to the sea. Imagine their feelings as the ship disappeared over the horizon, knowing they would not see him again. They did not know their spiritual father was on his way to martyrdom.

Paul's Travelogue

A feature of Luke's record is his careful charting of Paul's travels. You can take your Bible and a map and trace all of Paul's tours. From Miletus, the journey to Jerusalem was by way of Coos, Rhodes, Patara, Tyre, and Caesarea.

Paul and his companions, no doubt, made the most of the various stops by ministering to groups of Christians at each point. At Tyre there was a delay of 7 days while the long and tedious job of unloading and loading cargo took place. The week spent there was an experience of rich fellowship, culminating in a tender farewell at the seashore (21:5).

Warned

Before leaving, the great apostle heard again the prophetic message warning him of impending peril and imprisonment. In his farewell to the Ephesian elders he had said, "The Holy Ghost witnesseth in every city, saying that bonds and afflictions abide me" (20:23). He was going "bound in the spirit unto Jerusalem, not knowing" what would befall him (v. 22).

Leaving the disciples at Tyre, Paul and his companions sailed down the Syrian coast to Caesarea. His sea voyage ended here and he traveled by land from Caesarea to Jerusalem. The missionary party lodged for many days with Philip, the evangelist, one of the seven men who had been selected to help the apostles (6:5).

Still another warning about his visit to Jerusalem was given Paul. The Spirit gave a prophecy through Agabus, a prophet who had seen his prophecies fulfilled (21:10, 11; 11:28).

A Problem

These warnings given through God's servants

under the direction of the Spirit pose problems for some in the light of Paul's continued insistence on going to Jerusalem. There are those who believe Paul did wrong, others feel as strongly that he did not. Of one thing we are certain—on each occasion Paul's party and the local believers pled with him not to go. Paul replied to those at Caesarea, "What mean ye to weep and to break mine heart? for I am ready not to be bound only, but also to die at Jerusalem for the name of the Lord Jesus" (21:13). When it became clear he could not be dissuaded, they gave up and said, "The will of the Lord be done" (21:14).

It appears God revealed to others that Paul would be arrested and imprisoned if he went to Jerusalem. The Biblical record does not indicate that God gave Paul a personal command not to go. Neither does the Bible at any time indicate the Spirit will use others to give a person guidance that is contrary to what the Spirit has given him personally. It is always safe to let a prophetic utterance be a confirmation rather than personal direction.

Guard Your Pronouncements

We should accept this situation in the life of Paul as his friends did—"The will of the Lord be done." Should any be quick to claim infallible pronouncement on the rightness or wrongness of fellow believers, they ought to criticize only where God's Word criticizes. And they might well consider the Biblical admonition: "Therefore judge nothing before the time, until the Lord come, who both will bring to light the hidden things of darkness, and will make manifest the counsels of the hearts: and then shall every man have praise of God" (1 Corinthians 4:5). If Paul did wrong, he was accountable to God. And we too shall give account for our decisions.

Paul was dedicated to the will of God. He determined to continue to Jerusalem for

"He saw a hand they could not see
　Which beckoned him away;
He heard a voice they could not hear
　Which would not let him stay."

Jerusalem at Last

Paul's arrival in Jerusalem triggered a series of events that finally brought him to Rome. After presenting the apostles and elders with the offering that had been collected among the Gentile Christians, "Paul described in detail what God had done by means of his ministry among the Gentiles" (21:19, *Moffatt*). James and the Jerusalem brothers responded by giving glory to God.

Kind Treatment Short-lived

The warm reception was short-lived. The Jerusalem leaders advised Paul to clear up a commonly held misconception of his attitude toward Moses and the Law (21:21-26). He was asked to join a group of Nazarites who were about to complete their vows and make sacrifice in the temple. These young men were in need of someone to pay for the sacrifices which they could not afford. Paul agreed to this for it was not a compromise of principle or fundamental truths. And he always endeavored to become "all things to all men" that he might "save some" (1 Corinthians 9:19-22).

The fact remains, however, that despite Paul's generous act, he paid a price. His entrance into the temple infuriated visiting worshipers (non-Christian Jews) from Asia Minor who apparently recognized him through Trophimus of Ephesus. He was seized and beaten. But for the alertness and intervention of Roman soldiers he could well have been killed. His defense on the castle stairs (Acts 22:1-21) is a classic—the first of five apostolic defenses recorded in the concluding chapters of Acts.

Great Peril . . . Great Poise

Shackled with chains but dauntless and unafraid in the very face of death, Paul addressed the rabid mob. The scene was dramatic.

He reminded them he too had persecuted the Christians and felt toward them as the Jews now felt toward him. Anticipating the questions they would raise, he explained his change by testifying of his conversion and his call to bring the gospel to the Gentiles (22:21). At the mention of his call to preach to the Gentiles, the mob exploded.

Again the Roman officer intervened. He couldn't understand what infuriated the Jews. He decided to use the regular method of questioning—tie Paul to the whipping post and beat the truth out of him. Paul alerted the soldier to his Roman citizenship. The word was like magic. No Roman could be flogged without a trial and Paul was spared that horror (22:24-29).

Taken before the Sanhedrin the next day, and seeing no hope of justice being meted out to him, Paul set one part of that body against the other. He saw the crowd was made up of Pharisees and Sadducees, two religious parties who hated each other with a vengeance. The Sadducees rejected all the Scriptures except the law of Moses. In contrast with the Pharisees, they did not believe in angels, spirits, the resurrection, judgment, or future punishment. Declaring that he was a Pharisee and "of the hope and resurrection of the dead I am called in question" (23:6), the parties were very cleverly split as Paul summoned the support of the Pharisees on doctrinal grounds. The Sanhedrin became hopelessly divided. The contention was so violent the Roman officer feared Paul would be torn to pieces. He ordered his soldiers to take Paul by force back to the safety of the fort (23:9, 10).

12   Minister Extraordinary

Read: Acts 23:11 to 26:32

Many times it takes real courage to stand up and be counted; but to keep standing up after being counted is the real test of courage.

Taking a pencil, the teacher held it upright on the table. "Why doesn't this pencil fall?" he asked.

"Because you hold it up," was the student's reply.

"Yes, that's right," replied the teacher. "There's no power in the pencil itself, but an outside power holds it up."

Paul's life was one of continually standing up, not only to be counted, but also continuing to stand after being counted. He could never have stood so steadfastly if it had not been for the hand of the Almighty holding him up.

What Are Your Props?

Too many trust God only when the props of this world stand. When those props are knocked out from under them, they also collapse. They are like the woman in the buggy whose horses ran away with her. When asked afterward how she felt, she said, "Well, I trusted in God until the harness broke; then I shut my eyes and gave myself up for lost."

The Lord was with Paul in beatings, stonings, and imprisonment. He was there at his side when the mobs brought false charges against him and when legalistic brothers misunderstood him. God rescued him from more than one mob. When all the props seemed knocked away, God still stood with him. God does not expect any of us to stand in our own strength; He comes to us with an external power— himself. He'll hold the "pencil" upright.

Just Listening

Paul spent himself in action—preaching, pioneering, propagating, persevering. But he also spent a lot of time listening for God's word of guidance. If you'll take time to hear God through His Word and the impressions of the Spirit, you'll find comfort, encouragement, and guidance.

Following Paul's speech before the Sanhedrin, he was again thrown into prison. He was to spend a few days incarcerated in Jerusalem, then 2 years and 3 months at Caesarea, and more than 2 years at Rome. Imagine the ambitious, venturesome preacher now shackled in chains.

But, "The night following the Lord stood by him, and said, Be of good cheer, Paul: for as thou hast testified of me in Jerusalem, so must thou bear witness also at Rome" (23:11).

For years Paul had had the conviction he must someday witness in Rome (Romans 15:22-29). But the way things had been going since his arrival in Jerusalem, his plans were thwarted and his hopes appeared to be dashed. A howling mob shrieking for his life almost murdered him on the stairs of the fort (Acts 21:35). Later the Sanhedrin, which was to act always with dignity and decorum, erupted into mob violence and sought to tear him to pieces (23:10). What a far cry from a missionary tour to Rome!

"Don't worry, Paul; . . . you must also [tell the people about me] in Rome" (23:11, *The Living Bible).* A ruthless horde, a frustrated high priest (23:2), and a seething religious court could not defeat the will of God.

Trouble Brewing

But at the very time the Lord stood by Paul a new plot against him was brewing. They had not been successful in killing Paul in the temple or before the council. But they hadn't given up. A conspiracy was formed to get Paul out of the hands of the Romans and assassinate him.

More than 40 men bound themselves with an oath not to eat or drink until they had killed him (23:12). The malignant scheme, which had the sanction of the religious leaders, was to request that Paul be brought once again before the Sanhedrin for another hearing. The plotters proposed to ambush the soldiers, seize Paul, and kill him. How low these religious leaders had fallen! "The chosen people" planned murder! These men were acting in the name of religion, even as Paul had done before his conversion. Beware of misguided zeal!

But the plot failed. Be careful if you plan to oppose God and His servants. He has ways to bring to light the hidden things of darkness and dishonesty.

A Nameless Hero

Paul's nephew learned of the plot and rushed to Paul with the news. Paul sent him to tell the Roman commander of the threat on his life (23:16, 17). And the best laid plans of his enemies were again foiled.

This son of Paul's sister remains nameless as does the boy's mother. He must have been quite young, for three times he is spoken of as a "young man" (23:17, 18, 22). He appears on the scene suddenly, does his mission, and disappears as quickly into oblivion. Apart from this mention, we'd never know Paul had a sister or nephew. The nephew goes down in history as an important link in Paul's career by saving his life.

You may feel you are unknown and unheralded as was Paul's nephew, but somewhere there is a niche of service God has planned for you. Keep alert for your opportunity. It may never result in a news conference or a ticker-tape parade, but you'll hear the One with nail prints in His hands say, "Well done, good and faithful servant. . . ."

Escorted by the Military

Upon hearing the young man's report, the commander called two of his officers and told them to provide an army of 470 to accompany Paul from Jerusalem, protecting him from the assassins (23:23, 24). Of interest is the fact that Paul, who had trudged thousands of miles in the face of the greatest dangers, was now given a horse to ride and a military escort to protect him. And what about the some 40 men who took the oath not to eat or drink until they had killed Paul? Do you think they starved and dehydrated to death? Or did they break their vow?

Introduced to a Roman Ruler

Claudius Lysias, the commander, also sent a letter by which Paul secured a good introduction to Felix, the Roman judge. The letter related the story of Paul's unfair persecutions and the dangers to which he had been exposed, and by implication indicated the commander's belief as to Paul's innocence of the charges brought against him.

Upon reading the letter and hearing that Paul was a Roman citizen from Cilicia, the governor said, "I will hear you when your accusers arrive" (23:35, *TEV*). In the meantime, Paul was kept in the lavish palace built by Herod the Great.

Some might think that all was lost. Paul was a

prisoner, his ministry was halted, and his life was in jeopardy. We're prone to walk by sight and not by faith. Who would think the road to Rome would lead through Jerusalem? Now he was another step on his way to the imperial city he longed to visit.

On Caesarea

Caesarea, built by Herod the Great 22 years before the birth of Jesus, was the civil and military capital of Palestine. A great harbor, a mammoth amphitheater, a large theater, a lavish temple to Caesar Augustus, and colossal images honoring the emperor were all part of the massive spending program during the 12 years it took to build the city.

Significant events in the history of the Church took place there: The Spirit was first poured out on the Gentiles (10:1 to 11:18); Herod Agrippa I was struck with worms and died (12:21-23); Philip the Evangelist lived there (21:8); Agabus gave the final warning of Paul's impending imprisonment (21:10, 11); and Paul languished for 2 years in prison and made his defense on several occasions there (Acts 24 to 26). History records that during Paul's imprisonment the Jews and Gentiles clashed there and the Romans later massacred 20,000 Jews there. This event led to the destruction of Jerusalem in A. D. 70.

Paul was back in Caesarea after 5 days in Jerusalem. He was a prisoner of Rome. Luke devotes three chapters in Acts (24; 25; 26) to Paul's 2 years in Caesarea. Paul was not kept in close confinement and his friends were allowed to see him (24:23).

Seven Speeches

During this period, from Jerusalem to Rome, Paul made seven speeches that are recorded by Luke: (1) the speech before the mob in the temple (22:1-21), in which Paul told how he was changed from a persecutor to a believer; (2) the speech before the Sanhedrin (22:30 to 23:10) which brought confusion by raising the matter of the resurrection; (3) the speech before Felix, the Roman governor (24:10-22), in which he made his defense against Jewish accusers and affirmed his belief in the resurrection and in the "way which they call heresy"; (4) the speech before Felix and his wife Drusilla (24:24-27), where he "reasoned of righteousness, temperance, and judgment to come"; (5) the speech before Festus the Roman governor (25:7-11), in which he appealed to Caesar; (6) the speech before Festus, King Agrippa, and Bernice (25:13 to 26:32); and (7) the speech before the chief Jews in Rome (28:17-29), testifying that Jesus is the Christ and salvation is also for the Gentiles.

Time to Reflect

Significantly, Paul did no writing during his 2 years in Caesarea. Many scholars believe it was during this time that Luke, in frequent consultation with Paul, produced his first Book, the "former treatise" (Acts 1:1), which we know as the Gospel of Luke.

The 2 years spent in Caesarea were not wasted. No doubt Paul had time for reflection and contemplation. For over 20 years he had pushed forward against great odds in his missionary endeavors. Now he had a chance to rest. There is a difference to be noted in his writings following this period, although there is no contradiction or inconsistency. Romans and Galatians (written earlier) lay the foundation for Ephesians and Colossians which were penned later. As Stalker points out, in Paul's later letters he dwells less on the work of Christ and more on His person, and less on the justification of the sinner and more on the sanctification of the saint.

113

The Prosecutor Arrives

Five days after Paul's imprisonment in Caesarea, Ananias the high priest arrived in town with the elders and Tertullus, a lawyer who was to prosecute the case. Tertullus began his case with a buildup of unscrupulous flattery (24:2-4) and then proceeded to lodge the charge which was threefold: (1) Sedition—placing blame on Paul for the disturbances the Jews themselves had created; (2) Heresy—charging Paul with being a ringleader of the sect of the Nazarenes, a contemptuous term; (3) Sacrilege—profaning the temple. These were serious charges, especially that of instigating a revolt against Roman authority, which was punishable by death.

Paul's Defense

With courtesy and dignity Paul gave a straightforward account of the events of the last 12 days. He had come to the temple to worship the God of his fathers. The only difference between him and his accusers was he believed all that was written in the Law and the Prophets. Instead of being an offender, he always endeavored to live with a clear conscience (24:10-20).

On Felix

Felix was married to Drusilla, a Jewess who was the sister of King Agrippa and Bernice. Consequently, he knew something about the "way" (24:22). Felix was a cruel, lustful man. Tacitus, a Roman historian, wrote that Felix exercised the powers of a king in the spirit of a slave. His administration was so corrupt that 2 years later he was called before Nero and removed from office.

After hearing Paul, Felix postponed the trial for several days. Then he called for him again. This time his wife was present, and Paul preached the gospel—the *righteousness* of Christ, showing Felix his need of the Saviour; *temperance,* showing the necessity of godly self-denial and self-control, and exposing Felix's immorality and self-indulgence; *judgment* to come, reminding Felix that God would require him to give an account of his cruel torture and killing of thousands of people (24:24, 25).

Not Today

How did Felix respond? He *trembled* because his conscience was awakened. The Spirit showed him his guilt. He *procrastinated,* saying, "Go thy way . . . when I have a convenient season, I will call for thee" (24:25). There never was a convenient season for Felix and there never is for anyone. Now is the time.

Festus Comes on the Scene

Porcius Festus replaced Felix (this was the same office Pilate had held in Jesus' day) after 2 years. When Festus came to Jerusalem the leaders of the Jews brought Paul's case to him, accusing him as before. They petitioned to have Paul brought to Jerusalem for trial, although they secretly planned to kill him on the way. Festus refused to transfer Paul and after 10 days he went to Caesarea (25:1-6).

Paul Appeals to Rome

Paul was called before Festus in the judgment court. The Jerusalem Jews had arrived and immediately lodged several serious charges against Paul. The apostle responded by asserting his innocence of both treason against Caesar and of breaking the Jewish law by profaning the temple. When Festus suggested Paul return to Jerusalem to stand trial, the apostle reminded him that Caesarea was the proper place for the trial, that Festus knew he was not guilty, and that he would prove he was not guilty by appealing to Caesar (25:7-12). This right of appeal was a highly cherished right of Roman citizens which had been in effect since 509 B.C.

Enter King Agrippa

After Paul formally appealed his case, King Agrippa, a puppet ruler, with his consort-sister Bernice, paid a visit to Festus. Festus related Paul's case to Agrippa, explaining the charges were neither civil nor criminal but religious in nature, involving beliefs about "one Jesus" (25:13-19).

Agrippa's interest was aroused and he expressed a desire to listen to Paul. Accordingly, on the next day a state audience was arranged. Military leaders and dignitaries of the city were invited.

Festus appealed to Agrippa to investigate the case and help him decide what charges to specify against Paul in his bill of particulars to be sent to Caesar (25:20-27).

Paul was not required to defend himself before Agrippa for his appeal had been made to Rome, but he seized the opportunity to witness to this king who was part Jew by birth and all Jew by tradition. Agrippa was the son of Herod I who was eaten of worms (12:23). His marriage to his own sister Bernice was an incestuous, scandalous affair.

This was Paul's fifth defense. A master logician, his defenses reveal something of his character and ability. They are marked by straightforwardness, courtesy, eloquence, and compassion.

Paul's defense before Festus had been logical and he had demonstrated his accusers could not prove their charges (24:13, 19, 20). His appeal to Caesar (25:9-11) had been dramatic and final. But his address before King Agrippa at Caesarea was a fresh revelation of the nature and dynamic power of the gospel.

Representative Responses

Notice the responses of Festus and Agrippa. Festus shouted, "You are mad, Paul! Your great learning is driving you mad!" (26:24, *TEV*). He recognized Paul's intellectual attainments and spiritual passion. Without knowing it he paid tribute to the gospel but was unwilling to accept its truth.

Instead of finding himself listening to a cringing appeal for mercy or a flattering appeal for favor, Agrippa found himself on trial, pressed to make a decision for Christ. He uttered the famous words, "Almost thou persuadest me to be a Christian" (26:28). The word *Christian* is used only two times in Scripture (Acts 26:28; 1 Peter 4:16). If Agrippa had bypassed the "almost" of verse 28 to the "altogether" of verse 29, he would have known the joys of eternal life. And while King Agrippa is little known in history, Paul's name is a household word throughout the Christian world and beyond.

Festus, Agrippa, and Paul—each is representative of the response of people to the gospel. Festus, the rejector who declares the gospel as madness and folly. Agrippa, the one who either under conviction or in sarcasm turns from the gospel. Paul, the one who is convinced and surrenders to Christ. How important to obey "the heavenly vision" (26:19).

13 Rome at Last

Read: Acts 27 and 28

A man who was a golf enthusiast was telling another fellow how difficult it was, on a certain course, to drive a ball over a ditch that lay between the tee and the green. "Why don't they fill up the ditch?" asked the second man.

An older woman was watching a game of tennis, and saw how often the ball was driven against the net. "Why don't they take down the net?" was her question.

Paul's life was full of "ditches" and "nets." Five times he had received 39 stripes, three times he had been beaten with rods, once he had been stoned, and three times he had been shipwrecked. Often he had been in peril of robbers. Weary and in pain, in hunger and thirst, in cold and nakedness, his life was one of obstacles, hazards, and hindrances. Paul was as much at home in a jail as in a pulpit. What another would have found to be a stumblingblock was a stepping-stone to Paul (2 Corinthians 11:23-27).

He Feared Man So Little

Nothing moved Paul from his course. Nothing daunted him for a moment. Discouragement and depression were never evident. Howling mobs, unjust judges, determined Jews, scornful Greeks, haughty

Romans—their words and actions against him fell like water off a duck's back. False brethren, ungrateful churches, idolatrous cities, Felix, Festus, Agrippa, Nero—their deeds and words had no more effect on his determination than the cold spray against granite cliffs.

Oft but Not Soft

In journeys oft, but never soft, Paul endured "hardship, as a good soldier of Jesus Christ" (2 Timothy 2:3). And now he was about to begin his long journey to Rome. Through all of his "ditches" and "nets" he gave credence to the fact that the *soul would have no rainbow had the eyes no tears.*

All Roads Lead to Rome

That was more than a cliche in Paul's day. The Romans were noted for the roads they had built throughout the empire. And Paul was determined to "see Rome" (Acts 19:21); Rome had priority in his itinerary. Little did he know he would see his wish fulfilled in the way it all came about. To be taken on board ship as a prisoner, cast shipwrecked on an island after 2 weeks of storm, swim or drift to shore, and then spend 2 years under house arrest in Rome—what a way to see Rome! But through it all he was conscious of the presence of God, "whose I am, and whom I serve" (27:23).

Why Rome?

Why did Paul have this burning desire to "see Rome"? Two reasons can be given. One, because there was already a Christian church there and he longed to see the believers so he might impart some spiritual gift to them to the end that they might be established (Romans 1:11).

Second, Paul knew that while all roads *led to*

Rome, just as surely all roads *led from* Rome. This world center offered a prime target for spreading the gospel. Build the Church there and its influence would spread everywhere.

When Men Show Greatness

The last "we" section in Acts begins in chapter 27 as Luke traveled with Paul to Rome. The other companion was Aristarchus, a convert from Thessalonica, who became the apostle's fellow prisoner in Rome (Colossians 4:10). The record kept by Dr. Luke as an eyewitness is considered the most valuable document in existence concerning seamanship in ancient times. Luke, although not a sailor, used nautical terms with perfect accuracy. The space given in the narrative to the voyage suggests Luke considered it a very important event in Paul's life.

The experiences Paul went through en route to Rome give us a study in Christian maturity. His character sparkles in refreshing beauty despite events that would drive lesser men to near collapse. Consider these three dimensions of his maturity. *First,* he showed patience in the midst of hurry. *Second,* he manifested courage when others cowered in terror. *Third,* he maintained faith when others gave up in despair.

I'm in Partnership

Paul's serene confidence reminds me of the widow who was called on to raise a large family alone. A reporter, hearing of her unusual pluck, sought her out for a story. The first question was natural: "How have you been able to raise all these children and do it so well?"

"It's been very simple," the widow replied. "You see I'm in a partnership."

"A partnership? What kind of partnership?"

With a smile she answered, "One day a long time ago I said to the Lord, 'Lord, I'll do the work and You do the worrying,' and I haven't had a worry since."

This voyage, filled with extreme perils, required the utmost presence of mind and the ability to win the confidence and obedience of all on board. How remarkable that Paul, who was neither a soldier nor a sailor, became the dominant figure in the whole incident. Before reaching Rome, Paul was in essence both the captain of the ship and general of the soldiers. And all 276 persons aboard owed their lives to him.

The Historic Trip Begins

The first stage of the voyage was from Caesarea to Fair Havens in Crete. At Sidon, the kindly Roman army officer, Julius, permitted Paul to go ashore to visit friends. At Myra the company was transferred to a grain ship from Alexandria going to Italy (Egypt was Rome's granary). The voyage was continued in rough weather, the ship nearly foundering on the rocks of Salmone, but reaching Fair Havens in safety.

At Fair Havens, Paul urged Julius (the Roman army officer would have final authority) to have the ship remain during the winter to escape impending dangers (27:10). But the captain and owner of the ship wanted to winter in a more favorable harbor at Phoenix some 60 miles farther west. The experts said, "Let's take the risk." The crowd said, "Let's find a better spot than this dreary place to spend the winter." Julius listened to the experts and the crowd. He counted the votes instead of weighing the merits.

But the man who knew God was wiser than the men who knew the sea. Live in "the secret of the Lord" and you'll have the lead on those who depend on natural skills alone.

A Nightmare

The next 2 weeks became a nightmare. Misled by a soft wind blowing from the south, the men thought they could carry out their plan. But no sooner had they gotten out to sea than a tempestuous "northeaster" struck. Julius and the captain lost their gamble.

Five verbs describe not only the events that took place during the storm, but also the events in a person's life when he turns away from God's voice. First, the ship *loosed* from its moorings (27:13). Second, the ship was *caught* in a tempestuous wind (27:15). Third, the ship was *driven* in the storm (27:17). Fourth, the ship had to be *lightened* of its cargo (27:18). Fifth, the ship was *broken* on the rocks (27:41).

Standing in Bold Relief

Into this trying situation Paul stepped forward with a word from God. "Take courage! Not one of you will lose his life; only the ship will be lost" (27:22, *TEV*). The apostle stands out in bold relief. He practically took command. The captain took his advice; the crew took courage at his word; the sailors were prevented from cowardly desertion; and the lives of all the prisoners were saved (27:30-44).

The terrible experience was over. Exhausted and dripping, yet glad to be alive, sailors, soldiers, passengers, and prisoners struggled onto the beach, which they discovered to be the island of Melita (present-day Malta). Quickly a friendly crowd of the islanders gathered around the wet, shivering victims of the storm. A crackling fire was built for the escapees from a watery grave.

Safe ashore, Paul gathered sticks to throw on the fire. The man who could give orders could also take his share of responsibility. A poisonous snake fastened itself on his hand. Believing that Paul was a criminal who was being avenged by the gods, the superstitious islanders expected Paul to drop dead within minutes. Their apprehension turned to astonishment when the apostle didn't die. Surely, they said, he must be a god (28:3-6).

Luke records a second miracle that occurred during the 3 months (November, December, and January) they spent on Malta (28:7-10). The chief man on the island was a man named Publius. He extended 3 days of gracious hospitality to Paul and his companions. Paul found that Publius' father was very ill with a fever and dysentery. He laid his hands on him and the man was healed. The news spread and other sick people came and received healing. No doubt Paul and his friends were greatly used of the Lord during this time of enforced delay. When the time came to leave, the islanders showered the destitute voyagers with gifts of love, providing for their necessities.

Safe to Sail Again

Sailing was again safe and the whole company continued their journey to Rome in a ship similar to the one that had broken apart in the storm. The carved figures adorning it represented Castor and Pollux, supposedly the patron deities of sailors.

Luke's accurate recording (28:11-15) is noted as they journeyed on to Syracuse (the chief city of Sicily), Rhegium, and Puteoli (in the Bay of Naples), the leading port for Rome (140 miles away). Christians were discovered at Puteoli, and Paul and his friends remained with them for 7 days. Believers in Rome received word Paul was on his way. Some of them walked as far south on the Appian Way as Appii Forum (about 40 miles from Rome). Others met him at the Three Taverns (about 30 miles out of the city). Luke clearly states how heartwarming this demon-

stration of Christian love and concern was to Paul—
"Whom when Paul saw, he thanked God, and took
courage" (28:15).

Rome at Last

At last Paul's wish was fulfilled—he was in Rome.
And Caesar had paid the fare all the way from
Jerusalem! The drama begins to draw to a close. The
scene had opened in Jerusalem, the Holy City for the
Jews. But they had missed God's best. They had
called His Son a blasphemer, charged Him with
treason, and watched Him die on a cross to redeem
all who would believe on Him. But the grave could
not hold Him. He arose and appeared to His disciples, commanding them to wait for His promise of
the Holy Spirit.

The small nucleus of 120 who were endued with
the power of the Spirit in the Upper Room mush-
roomed into a dynamic body whose impact was
made on almost every major city of the Roman Empire.

Throughout the Book of Acts the missionary
movement had been gaining momentum and moving toward a climax in Rome. What God had wrought
in Jerusalem, the Holy City, Paul brought to Rome,
the Imperial City.

What Did Paul See in Rome?

"I must see Rome" had been Paul's earnest desire.
Now Rome at last and what did he see?

He found the cruel, merciless, 25-year-old emperor, Nero. Nero's hands were already stained with
blood and in a few years he would be "playing his
fiddle while Rome burned."

He found a great city. Rome was a city of 2 million
people of whom half were slaves. The paupers were
forever crying for free bread or for entertainment at

the circus where gladiators fought wild animals and each other to entertain the masses.

He found a Christian community large enough to be known and despised by pagan Rome. Many of them were already paying the price for their Christian testimony as they became martyrs in the circus.

He found many Jews—perhaps 40,000. They had returned after their banishment by Claudius years before (18:2). For these, Paul's brethren in the flesh, his great heart ached and yearned.

At last in Rome—but he was chained to a soldier, one of the famous Praetorium Guard. He was, however, a privileged prisoner, a Roman citizen who had claimed his right to have his case heard by the emperor. Under constant guard, he was permitted to live in rented quarters with no restrictions to visitors.

Who Came to See Paul?

Paul's quarters became the scene of intense activity for his Lord and Saviour. A stream of visitors entered the doors of his abode. Who were they?

First, came Roman Jews at Paul's invitation just 3 days after his arrival. To these he preached the gospel. "Some believed ... and some believed not" (28:24).

Second, Christian friends, some of whom he was meeting for the first time, and others who had sat under his ministry elsewhere. Romans 16 lists the names of many.

Third, his personal friends of long standing. Among these were Luke and Aristarchus (28:16; Colossians 4:10, 14), Aquila and Priscilla (Romans 16:3-5). Timothy and Tychicus, Mark and Onesimus, Epaphras and many others (Colossians 4:7-14). They came to encourage him and to drink from the well of his wisdom. Some helped him in his letter writing;

others became messengers to bear his letters to distant points.

Fourth, there were the guards. Some of these became converts, thus bringing the penetration of the gospel to the palace and Caesar's household (Philippians 1:13; 4:22).

Impossible, But . . .

Rome exercised worldwide dominion. With its fabulous wealth, unchallenged sovereignty, arrogant might, and complacent self-sufficiency, the task of gaining a foothold for the gospel seemed impossible. For the job of storming this seemingly impregnable citadel God sent a prisoner—a man in chains with a body racked with pain and weakened by innumerable privations and backbreaking travel and work; a man from a despised race who was charged with a crime! Possibly that man accomplished as much in those 2 years of imprisonment as in any 2 years of his freedom. Never did he count himself a prisoner of Rome, but of Christ (Philippians 1:12, 13).

Slaves were converted. Nobles and highborn women were led into newness of life. Soldiers carried the message as they served their legions throughout the empire.

In his "hired house" Paul had time for thought and reflection. For us the great results are the Prison Epistles—Philippians, Colossians, Ephesians, and Philemon. God arranged for Paul to be kept in Rome at Caesar's expense and the treasures of these Epistles became the heritage of the Church. How we are enriched by them!

Acts Has No Customary "Amen"

The Book ends with Paul in his own house, though a prisoner, receiving all who came to him and preaching and teaching. Why does Acts end so abruptly? Why didn't Dr. Luke tell us what happened at the trial? Something about Paul's martyrdom? The Book may seem to have no formal ending, but that was what the Holy Spirit directed. God wants to impress on us that there is no conclusion to "all that Jesus began . . . to do" (1:1) as long as the Church is in the world. Acts begins with the unfinished work of Christ and ends with the unfinished work of Paul, the Church, and the Holy Spirit.

Where Luke's narrative ends, tradition offers some information. It is generally believed Paul was tried before Nero and acquitted. Tradition tells us he resumed his travels and visited even far-off Spain. From a careful study of his epistles, we do feel with certainty that he traveled widely, but only for a brief period. Before long Paul was imprisoned in Rome. No longer was it a "hired house," but a dungeon. From this place—the worst known to law—Paul wrote his second letter to Timothy. First Timothy and Titus were written between his imprisonments.

Read 2 Timothy and you are gripped with the unspeakable pathos. No one was with him, save the Lord who stood by him. Stalker writes:

> The trial ended, Paul was condemned and delivered over to the executioner. He was led out of the city with a crowd of the lowest rabble at his heels. The fated spot was reached; he knelt beside the block; the headsman's axe gleamed in the sun and fell; and the head of the apostle of the world rolled down in the dust (James Stalker, *Life of St. Paul* [Old Tappan, NJ: Fleming H. Revell, 1912], p. 148).

The close of Paul's life is in a sense veiled from our eyes, but no cloud can ever dim the splendor of the services that life rendered for God and us.